WHAT'S DONE
in the
SHADOWS

A SEDUCTIVE THRILLER

MONIQUE
ELISE
PUBLICATIONS

WHAT'S DONE *in the* SHADOWS

A SEDUCTIVE THRILLER

MONIQUE ELISE

ALSO BY
Monique Elise:

Dilemmas of a Damel: Part One
Dilemmas of a Damsel: Part Two
Dilemmas of a Damsel: Part Three
Red Echo

DEDICATION

I dedicate this book to the ones I have lost during its creation. The loss of a loved one is never easy, and there were many moments when I was consumed by grief. Yet, something deep within me kept pushing me to see this project through. I know it's because of the guardian angels who continue to watch over me.

To my beloved grandfather, Heriberto "Rocco" Colon Jr., my poppop — losing you was the hardest thing I've ever endured. Thank you for loving me, protecting me, guiding me, and always being so supportive of my creative endeavors. I'll never forget how proud you were when I first embarked on this journey as an author, and how eager you were to share my books with your friends. You were so excited to buy my books and hand them out to everyone you knew. I will forever cherish your unwavering support. I will love you forever and a day, and until we meet again, I will continue to do all I can to make you proud.

To my cousin, Amirah Hatton, whose beauty and light were undeniable — you were taken from us far too soon. I don't think I will ever find the right words to truly capture how divine you were and how deeply you touched the lives of everyone around you. Watching you blossom from a young girl into a mother warmed my heart immensely, and I wish I could have told you just how proud I always was of you. Though I miss you terribly, I find comfort in knowing that you are now reunited with your baby boy, Isa. Thank you for teaching me the importance of slowing down, finding beauty in everything, and encouraging me to dream big. I'm done holding back, cousin! I love you girl, until we meet again…

"The greatest battle we face as human beings is the battle to protect our true selves from the self the world wants us to become."

-E. E. Cummings

PROLOGUE

Click.
Clack.
Click. Clack.
Click.
Clack.

The pace of her swift steps echoes through the night. She tries her best to maintain her composure as she navigates the uneven pavement and chipped gravel in her heels. For in the heart of the city, where the neon signs and streetlights cast long shadows over dimly lit alleyways, lies a world covered in secrets and deception. Danger lurks around just about every corner, waiting to find its next victim. In this world, the line between right and wrong is often blurred.

All too familiar with navigating the precariousness of living in Philadelphia, she moves through the gritty streets with the stealth of a shadow. Her senses are on high alert when she notices a dark car that rounds the corner just a few yards behind. She keeps a steady stride in her step as a delicate sense of unease prickles at the back of her neck. Causing her eyes to periodically cast sly glances over her shoulder, checking her surroundings. Each time that she does, the car seemingly inches closer and closer. The air grows thick with tension, suffocating in its silence. She quickens her pace, every step pounding like a drumbeat in the quiet of the night.

Click.

Clack. Click.

Clack. Click.

Clack.

Suddenly, a shadowy figure emerges from the darkness, pursuing her like a predator stalking its prey. Her heart pounds as she breaks into a desperate run, the sound of heavy footsteps echoing in her ears. Panic surges through her as she darts down narrow side streets, her breath coming in ragged, uneven gasps as she tries to outrun her pursuer. She wants to yell, to call for help, but the thick, suffocating fog chokes the words in her throat. To her horror, the figure remains hot on her heels, closing in with every stride.

And then, without warning, they're upon her. A hand reaches out, grabbing her hair from behind and applying pressure to her throat. They forcibly pull her into the suffocating embrace of the waiting car. Her screams are muffled by a cloth clamped over her nose and mouth. She tries to fight them off, but they're too strong, making her struggles useless against the overwhelming force that binds her.

Then she feels it. Her head grows foggy, making it hard to separate dreams from reality. She tries her hardest to stay present, knowing that if she doesn't, she'll be lost forever. In the blink of an eye, her world is plunged into darkness, and her consciousness goes black. With her fate uncertain, she's swiftly whisked away into the night.

CHAPTER

One

DESTINED PATHS

Jada

August 2003

Vibrant hues of amber and gold paint a hypnotizing picture behind my closed eyelids, each warm ray of sunlight feeling like a gentle kiss against my skin. With my head tilted back, I allow a soft sigh to escape my lips, completely surrendering to the embrace of the August summer sun. Although I know that these few seconds of peace will soon come to an end, it feels as though, during this moment, time stands still, and I could be here forever.

Unfortunately, reality quickly settles in like an annoying flicker of dust. I'm instantly reminded that the perfection of summertime bliss must soon give way to the realities of life.

The first days of my ninth-grade year haunt my thoughts. I inhale sharply, trying my hardest to push aside the nagging reminder. I'd much rather spend the last days of summer break losing myself in the kaleidoscope of my daydreams.

There, I'm transformed into a vision of glamour and success, strutting down catwalks adorned in couture and expensive jewelry. I rival some of the greatest supermodels like Tyra Banks or Naomi Campbell. My husband, a powerhouse in the music industry, stands by my side. Together, we happily explore the globe, make award show appearances, and visit our homes sprinkled across every continent.

Just then, the faint ringing out of police sirens warps me back into the real world. I reluctantly open my eyes, allowing the allure of my coming escape to finally give way. I stare at the colorful, faded graffiti on the concrete wall across the street. The promise of a brighter future beyond the confines of North Philly slipping away from me. I use my hand to wipe away the tiny beads of sweat that have now formed across my forehead. My lips part slightly, letting out another sigh. This has to be one of the hottest days of the season.

Despite the heat, the block is lively. The dope dealers hang in front of the neighborhood corner store while older residents gather on their decorated porches to converse and share memories of the good ole days, all with watchful eyes, of course. A car parked illegally in front of a fire hydrant loudly blasts "Frontin" by Pharell Williams from its speakers, its base vibrating throughout the neighborhood. Some yards away, a soft bell hums, indicating the arrival of the local ice cream man.

I rise up from my stoop and walk to grab a popsicle, desiring something sweet to beat the summer heat. As I stroll along the sun-coated concrete, the rhythmic sound of jump ropes clapping against the street fills the air, punctuated by the chatter and giggles of girls engaged in a game of double dutch. Their synchronized movements are a testament to years of practiced skill, pausing only briefly to make way for the passing cars that disrupt their play.

Meanwhile, school boys whiz past on their bicycles, their laughter mingling with the hum of spinning wheels as they try to outdo each other with daring stunts. Dust clouds form under their tires as they race down the street, their youthful energy a vibrant backdrop to the afternoon.

Once I reach the ice cream truck, the attendant, an older Black man donning a sleeveless undershirt and Panama straw hat, smiles, "What can I get you, chica?" His Spanish accent entwined with his words.

"A cherry freeze pop, please," I say.

"That'll be fifty cents."

As he gathers my order, I reach into the pocket of my denim shorts and pull out two silver quarters. He holds his large hand out, which is decorated with an assortment of chunky gold rings. I place the money into his palm before he passes me my popsicle. Pleased, I proceed back to my porch, using the edges of my teeth to rip off the plastic covering so that I can start sucking the cold melted juice out. As I do, I see the crowd around the double dutch girls has gotten larger. I spot Fatima, a friendly girl from school, along with Cherelle, her loud and rowdy friend who dresses two sizes too small for her figure. I roll my eyes and keep to myself, passing by the clique. I don't have many friends, but I don't mind. After all, I don't plan on staying here much longer. Momma promised me we'd be together soon, and she would be coming to get me any day now.

"Hey, Jada! Do you want to come to the courts with us? They're about to start the games," Fatima calls out from across the street.

Her smile beams as she crosses the street to join me, her auburn brown skin glowing and her hair neatly tucked under her hijab. I shake my head in refusal. Going to the courts was just code for watching and flirting with the older boys playing basketball.

"Aw, why not? It'll be fun!" Fatima pleads, her enthusiasm contagious.

"I have to finish my chores," I offer as an excuse, though it's a lie.

The truth is, I have no interest in competing for the attention of those boys or engaging in anything remotely similar. Fatima understands this, knowing all too well the strictness of her own parents and the risks involved. I'm shocked that she'd even take the chance, but I keep my reservations to myself. Just then, Cherelle approaches, joining us.

"Don't lie, Jada. You know your mom won't let you go anywhere," Cherelle taunts, her words laced with cruelty. She pauses, her index finger tapping her cheek thoughtfully. "Oh, wait, I forgot, you don't have a mom," she adds with a smirk.

Another thing I can't stand about Cherelle is her insatiable appetite for bullying.

My eyes shoot daggers at her. "Yes, I do," I retort, my voice trembling with suppressed anger.

I can feel the rage bubbling within me, but I know better than to escalate the situation. The last thing I need is to get in trouble again for fighting, so I choose to walk away. Seeking solace, I retreat to my porch and settle onto the top step, further peeling off the wrapping of my popsicle to find some semblance of peace.

However, my refuge is short-lived. My stomach sinks as I watch Cherelle approach, now flanked by her gang of followers.

"Well, where is she then?" Cherelle demands, her hands planted firmly on her hips. "All the kids in this house are unwanted strays. And last time I checked, this is where you live."

Her friends all giggle in the background, encouraging her.

"Come on, Relle, leave her alone," Fatima pleads.

Cherelle turns to her, "Shut up, Fatima, damn!"

I never understood why Fatima would be friends with someone so malicious. In the six months since I moved here, all I've seen was Cherelle's wrath toward her, too. Fatima quickly looks to the gravel beneath her feet. She wasn't a fighter, and I never judged her for it. In fact, I've come to admire it, but sometimes I wish she'd stand up for herself.

By now, Cherelle directs her venomous gaze back toward me. With deliberate steps, she closes the distance between us, and I rise to my feet, bracing myself for confrontation. Cherelle made it her business to be the loudest, meanest person wherever she went. It's like she hated the world and made it her personal vendetta to make everyone around her miserable. I am almost certain that the only reason Cherelle is popular is that she intimidated everyone at school… except me.

"Besides, she won't do shit," she challenges.

My skin prickles with fury as she dares to reach out with one of her hands, poised to touch a strand of my hair—bangs that I had painstakingly styled for nearly an hour, inspired by the singer Mya's popular look.

"We're going to miss the game, y'all," Fatima says, the worry thick in her delivery.

But it's too late. This time, I'd had enough. It was time to put this dog down.

I retaliate, my words cutting through the tension. "Why don't you take your miserable behind somewhere else, Cherelle? You're always trying to bully someone, but face it, you're only doing that because you don't like who you are. You know you're ugly, inside and out. That's why you're so jealous of me."

A murmur of agreement ripples through the now-growing crowd, spurred on by my defiance. I see a flicker of anger in Cherelle's eyes, a sign that I've hit a nerve.

"Whatever, Jada. You think you're so much better than everyone just because you have nice hair. What do you think, you're Puerto Rican or something?" she snaps back, her tone dripping with disdain.

"Maybe you think I'm better than you since you're always checking for me," I shoot back, rolling my eyes in exasperation.

The tension between us escalates, fueled by the murmurs of onlookers egging us on. Cherelle, never one to back down, steps closer, sizing me up with a challenging glare.

"You must want to get your ass beat," she threatens.

Ever since I moved here, I've made sure to keep it cool and stay out of trouble. Cherelle isn't the first bully I've dealt with; they're all the same. Normally, I don't let them get to me, but today was not the day. I was going to have to teach this girl a serious lesson, especially before we began high school. It was now or never. Although my mother taught me never to go looking for a fight, she always told me to defend myself if one comes my way. It's a rule for survival, and I'm a survivor.

I cross my arms over my chest, "I bet you won't."

Thick tension coats the air as a brief moment of silence lingers between the two of us, each waiting to see who will make the first move. Then, with my peripheral vision, I see her fingers gather into a tight grip. But before Cherelle can swing, I pull my hand back with a clenched fist and punch her in the mouth with all my might. It's a clean hit, the impact so loud it takes everyone by surprise. In an instant, I see her eyes water. By the look on her face, I could tell she knew that she'd played this all wrong. For she had finally met her match.

"Damn, Relle, you gonna let her do you like that?" one of her friends says, clearly shocked by my bravery.

Cherelle wipes the blood from her lips and charges forward, trying to tackle me to the ground. By now, the crowd had tripled in size, attracting attention from all that were nearby. The neighborhood kids loved watching two girls go at it. This was their version of a live pay-per-view action fight. In normal cases, they were used to seeing Cherelle get the best of whoever her victim was, but not today. Her attack was wild and sloppy in comparison to my smooth and deliberate barrage of punches. The boxing training I received from my granddaddy before he died never steered me wrong. My hands and stamina were just too fast for her, and she was taking a serious beating. Just as I was preparing to land another jab, I was being grabbed by a pair of strong hands.

"Break it up, break it up," a deep voice says with an authority that no one would dare question.

I quickly realize it's Mr. Lewis, the owner of the recreation center just around the corner, and makeshift father figure to the kids in the area. With the help of one of his employees, they're able to pull Cherelle and me apart.

As the crowd dissipates, Cherelle points a finger at me, her hair now a tangled mess, her nose bloody, and her left eye swollen, "This isn't over, bitch."

"Get out of here and stop causing so much trouble, Cherelle," Mr. Lewis scolds.

Once I gather myself, Mr. Lewis sets his eyes on me with a hint of disapproval, which causes me to panic. The last thing that I needed was to get caught up in any trouble. And given how friendly Mr. Lewis was with my foster mother, I knew that I'd severely screwed up. I've been to a lot of group homes, and this one is the best by far. Even though I'm counting down the days that I can be reunited with my mother again, I can't risk being thrown out before that happens. I actually like it here. Impulsively, I want to curse myself for my bad judgment. Luckily for me, Ms. Gwen is extremely patient and kind. I just hope this time will also be the case.

Gwendolyn Cooper, or Ms. Gwen, for all intents and purposes, is my foster mother. She is a gentle yet stern woman who opened her home to many children like me. Ms. Gwen has been very nice, but I always noticed the sadness in her eyes. I once heard her husband got sick with some virus back in the day and died, leaving her heart forever broken. She couldn't have children of her own, and instead of turning cold on the world, she does her best to give a home to kids that otherwise wouldn't have one. Of course, this dedication does not leave much room for a love life, but Mr. Lewis still tries.

As Cherelle and her gang of followers retreat, seemingly defeated, I quickly touch my face, trying to assess the damage. To my relief, my skin still feels soft to the touch. I snort to myself. That girl barely laid a finger on me.

"Are you okay?" Mr. Lewis asks.

I nod. "I didn't want to fight her, but she's been bullying me. I figured it's best to put an end to it before school starts."

He grins, a nostalgic flash of childhood games and feuds playing in his mind. "Defending yourself is honorable, but next time, get an adult," he advises.

"Yes sir," I nervously look down, staring at my tennis shoes.

Mr. Lewis places his hand on my shoulder. "Don't worry. This will stay between us so long as it doesn't happen again. Now, go home and put some ice on those fists, Rocky."

I smile and go back to sitting on my porch. There were only a few left lingering from all the raucous. Luckily, things had quickly died down, and Ms. Gwen hadn't come outside. A few kids approach me, singing my praise and showing admiration for someone finally taking down the big bad monster.

"Dang, you beat her up bad, Jada. Where'd you learn to fight like that?" Aigne', my younger foster sister, asks.

I respond, "My poppop, he was an amateur boxer back in the day."

"Can you teach me?" she asks.

I giggle at her eagerness. She was barely ten years old and already trying to be grown.

"You don't need to be worried about fighting, Aigne'. But you should be able to stand up for yourself. No one likes bullies. Remember that," I explain.

She nods and smiles before going into the house and turning to me, "Don't worry, I won't tell her you were fighting."

I give her a wink and re-adjust my ponytail. Once I do, a Gray Oldsmobile pulls up in front. When I peer into the vehicle, I see a familiar face, Ms. Watkins, our social worker. My eyes travel to the back seat of the car and see a girl who looks to be about my age.

"Hello, there, Jada," Ms. Watkins says as she gets out of the car, her floral dress sticking to her back with sweat.

"Hey, Ms. Watkins," I say, rising to my feet and digging my hands into my back pockets.

She helps the girl out of the car, and the two approach the stoop. I continue to eye them with curiosity as the girl keeps her gaze on the ground. The girl clings to her duffle bag as if she's holding on for dear life.

She smiles, "How are things going around here? Are you staying out of trouble?"

I nod. "Yes, ma'am.' Have you heard from my mom yet?"

She touches my shoulder, "No, no new news yet, honey, but when I get some, you'll be the first to know. In the meantime, I have someone for you to meet. This is Tempest. She's going to be staying here for a while. I want you to ensure that she's welcomed, okay?"

I lock eyes with the scrawny girl who looks like a deer caught in headlights. Her hair is matted, and her glasses are bent all out of shape.

"Yes, ma'am," I reply.

Great, just what we need, another kid in this house.

Tempest

MUFFLED ECHOES OF SCREAMS RING OUT IN MY EARS, AN UN-pleasant, screeching sound imprinted on my mind. Vivid memories of things I'd like to forget continuously plague my thoughts. I quickly open my eyes, sleep eluding me once again, like a fleeting dream slipping through my fingers. I lie in bed, choosing to focus on the cracked ceiling above. But instead of the imperfections serving as a distraction from my suffering, the peeling paint chips are a stark reminder of the fractured state of my existence. It's been only two days since I found myself thrust into this unfamiliar place, a temporary sanctuary that offers little comfort amid the turmoil raging within.

Despite the relative snugness of my surroundings, a nagging feeling of longing for home claws at my chest. It is a relentless ache that refuses to be soothed. The weight of my displacement bears down upon me like a heavy blanket, suffocating any promise of peace.

I can hear Ms. Gwen's voice vibrate through the house, a melodic symphony among the constant chaos. The patter of little feet echoes down the hallway as her foster children race through the house, their laughter a joyful crescendo that fills the air. Despite the whirlwind of chatter and activity, Ms. Gwen moves with a sense of calm assurance, effortlessly balancing the needs of her bustling household.

Since my arrival, I've carefully observed her, eager to learn more about the woman who would be my guardian for the foreseeable future. I couldn't help but be amazed at her ability to navigate the tumultuous waters of foster care with such grace and poise. Yet, even as I admire her strength, I am keenly aware of the stark contrast between her world of warmth and love and the cold, stiff reality that is my new life.

Deep in the depths of my despair, I'm consumed by a storm of emotions—anger, fear, grief, and sorrow swirling together in a cyclone of anguish. I long to unleash the well of tears that threaten to overwhelm me, to scream out in defiance against the cruel hand fate has dealt me. But I am paralyzed by the knowledge that my cries will go unheard.

So far, I've managed to blend in without drawing too much attention to myself. I clutch my novel between my trembling hands, its pages a fragile lifeline. With a quivering breath, I immerse myself in its world, seeking refuge from the relentless onslaught of my thoughts and fears. As I strive to lose myself in the words printed on the page, my thoughts betray me once more, wandering to the uncertain future that lies ahead.

Will I be forgotten and left here to rot?

Who will love me now?

What does my future hold?

I quickly shut my eyes and silently pleaded with the universe, clinging to the hope that one day, my prayers would be answered and that I wouldn't be alone. But before I can whisper an "Amen," the door creaks open, disrupting my pleas. Standing in the doorway is Jada, my roommate, her expression a mixture of curiosity and perhaps a hint of annoyance. After all, who would willingly share their space with a stranger?

Our cramped bedroom, barely two hundred square feet, somehow manages to accommodate two twin-sized beds and matching chests of drawers. In one corner, a modest television rests atop a wooden stand, its flickering screen a distraction from the sharp reality of our shared confinement. The walls, painted a dull eggshell color, are adorned with an array of posters on Jada's side of the room. Supermodels and R&B icons gaze down at me from their glossy frames, a constant reminder of the contrast between our worlds. I long to be back in my own room, surrounded by the collectibles, maps, and books that have become my haven.

I try to focus on my book as she enters the room and closes the door behind her. Before she reaches her bed, she turns to me, her expression focused as if deliberately weighing her next words.

"You wanna go to the mall?" she asks, catching me off guard.

Instinctively, I shake my head no in response.

She scoffs, her frustration clear, "Seriously? Do you do anything besides lay in bed all day, buried in books? Who reads during summer, anyway? Especially with school right around the corner."

I sit up, offering a nonchalant shrug. "It helps me pass the time."

"What are you reading?" Her curiosity piques as she joins me at the foot of the bed, a hint of genuine interest in her tone.

"Along Came a Spider," I say, showing her the cover.

I watch as her eyes scan over the cover, "A detective, huh? You wanna be a cop or something?"

I shrug, "I don't know, maybe."

Truthfully, I just wanted to survive ninth grade—another dreadful reminder of what's in store. I wasn't looking forward to it.

Jada shrugs. "That's cool, I guess. I don't think I know any cops who look like you, though. My momma said don't ever trust the po-po, but she doesn't know everything. If she did, she wouldn't get into so much trouble all the time."

Her confidence makes me nervous. I avoid making eye contact, instead pulling on a loose hem on my sweatshirt.

She settles onto her bed, facing me with a momentary pause. "Why don't you wanna come to the mall? There's a bookstore by the food court you can check out."

Her conviction is admirable, making it hard to resist her offer. "Okay," I reply, a hint of uncertainty coloring my tone.

Her smile grows at my acceptance, but I can sense her scrutinizing me once more, her gaze making me feel uncomfortably self-conscious.

"What?" I ask, attempting to mask my unease with nonchalance.

"I'm sorry, but we've got to do something about your hair. It's a hot mess. When's the last time you combed it?" she remarks, her concern evident in her voice.

I shrug, a pang of embarrassment creeping in. "Honestly, I can't remember."

"Don't take this the wrong way. I can't let you go outside looking like this; the boys would never stop picking on you, especially with you being dark-skinned. You'd never hear the end of it."

My eyes focus on my dirty sneakers, unsure of her capability to handle the task at hand.

"Don't worry. My momma taught me how to do hair. She had her own beauty salon and everything," she says with pride.

"Okay," I say, still unsure.

"Come on," she says, grabbing my hand and pulling me out of my bed.

We step out into the hallway filled with rowdy kids, and she drags me to the bathroom at the end of the corridor. Once inside, she reaches for a towel, neatly folded in the linen closet, and expertly lays it on the floor next to the bathtub.

"Get down," she instructs.

"Huh?"

"If you can't remember the last time that you combed your hair, I know you ain't wash it," she says.

"Oh," I say.

She has a point. I had to agree with her observation. I carefully drop down to my knees. As I do, she turns the faucet knobs, toggling between hot and cold water, periodically testing the water with her fingers before finding the right temperature.

"All right, so bend your head under the water and keep your eyes shut. I mean it, or else soap is gonna get in them, and it's gonna hurt," Jada instructs.

I can't help but marvel at her confidence and the way she exudes assurance in every word she speaks. It's astounding for a fourteen-year-old girl, especially when I can barely stomach the thought of starting at a new high school. The mere idea makes me want to retreat beneath my bedcovers and wait until the school year is over.

Nevertheless, I follow her instructions and allow the warm water to hydrate my thick tresses. I feel her fingers working through my hair, skillfully untangling the knots and letting the water cascade over my kinky curls.

"You start school next week?" she asks.

I nod. "Yes, ninth grade."

She beams. "Oh, me too! You're probably going to Lincoln High like me. We can be friends."

The words leave her lips with so much promise. Although she's quite different from any of the friends I've had before, which is not many, it feels good knowing that I'm not alone, in this at least. The sound of the shampoo squirting into her palms signals the beginning of her cleansing process. Jada's hands move with expertise, massaging my scalp and lathering the shampoo into a rich foam. She scrubs away the build-up. Surprisingly, her touch feels comforting against my skin, kind of like my mother's. For a moment, I squeeze my eyes shut, pretending that Jada's hands are hers.

"Dang, you got some thick hair. It's really pretty, though," she remarks as she rinses away the dirt and suds.

She reaches for more shampoo, repeating the process with practiced ease. I force a smile. Mom used to say the same thing. She loved the ritual of washing and styling my hair every Sunday. That was before…

No, I can't let those memories resurface. I panic and open my eyes, only to be met with a stinging sensation of shampoo suds entering them.

"Ah!" I cry out in pain.

"Why'd you open your eyes? I told you to keep them closed!" Jada scolds.

In a panic, I reach out my hands, cupping the water into my palms and eagerly splashing it into my face for relief. I do this a few more times until the pain finally subsides. When I'm done, Jada hands me a fresh hand towel and watches me with curiosity as I dry my face, her arms crossed inquisitively across her chest.

"What's your story?" she presses, her tone gentle yet probing.

For a moment, I hesitate, the weight of my past heavy on my shoulders.

"If you're in here, you've got one. We all do," Jada says, her voice soft but certain.

As the water drips down my neck, I stare at her, unsure and scared of revealing my truth. But then I remember Jada's kindness, her promise of friendship, and her genuine attempt to welcome me into this new place. So, I find the courage to speak.

"I…" My voice falters, the words catching in my throat. I've never verbalized it before, never faced the truth head-on. But Jada offers a reassuring smile, a silent acknowledgment of shared pain and resilience she'd also likely endured. And so, with a deep breath, I finally confess, "I killed my parents."

CHAPTER

Two

THE ARRANGEMENT

Jada

STORMY

Present Day

My gaze sweeps across the inky stretch of the night sky. As a veil of darkness cloaks the cool autumn air, an enigmatic aura fills the night. With each passing moment, the evening fog thickens, covering the vacant lot with an eerie blanket of mystery. I sit in the driver's seat of my late model BMW, my fingers tracing the outline of my favorite bold crimson-red lipstick. In the reflection of the rearview mirror, my russet brown eyes gleam with a hint of anticipation.

At night, the old Navy Shipyard stands as a silent sentinel, its once lively docks now a ghostly graveyard for forgotten remnants of the past. The shadows of decaying battleships cast large silhouettes along the cold, murky water. This secluded corner of the world, bathed in dim, flickering lights, feels worlds away from the familiar excitement of the city.

As I wait in the stillness, a glint of movement in the distance suddenly catches my attention. Ahead, a faint glow of headlights pierces through the darkness. With an anxious breath, I sink back into the plush embrace of my heated leather seat, my heartbeat quickening with suspense. Tonight, amid the gloom of this quiet shipyard, a secret meeting is about to unfold.

My eyes quickly glance down to the space between my driver's seat and center console, the handle of my small handgun slightly peeking out. I take another deep, calming breath and carefully watch as the luxury car pulls up beside mine. I watch with caution as its driver shifts the car into park and powers it off. Moments later, my visitor steps out of the vehicle. As she does, memories of our initial meeting quickly flash before me, her proposition taking me completely by surprise.

"Let me get this straight." I pause. "You want to pay me to fuck your husband?"

Quinn nods, her eyes hard and unwavering, making it clear she is resolute in her decision. Her bluntness leaves my mouth dry. I reach for my dirty martini, placing the brim of the glass to my lips, pondering her request. Goodness, these wealthy folks are so strange. Their uncanny kinks and requests never cease to amaze me. Over the years, I've learned not to judge. After all, it's my job to provide a fantasy and cash in, but sometimes, their logic gives me complete pause.

I'm most certain that I've bedded plenty of married men. In fact, those are my favorites simply because they have much more at stake. Whether it be their reputation, wives, or seemingly perfect lives. The threat of losing something gives me leverage in this game, and it's something I've gotten quite comfortable using to my advantage. However, this is the first time I've had a man's spouse make such a daring request.

"Who is your husband?" I inquire.

Her jawline tenses as she reaches into her clutch and pulls out a single photograph, placing it on the table and sliding it toward me. I study the picture for a moment and quickly recognize the man staring back at me. His intense green eyes and playboy smile were unforgettable. We'd spent hours just a few nights before flirting relentlessly. It took little more than a glance for him to succumb to my allure; men often struggle to resist the pull of my tantalizing beauty. We'd exchanged numbers, and I was eager to get acquainted as I was in search of a new sponsor. Clay Winthrop, a prominent real estate mogul, was seemingly the perfect catch. This man seemed more than capable, offering me the moon and the stars. Something I was quite happy to receive. I just don't think he ever accounted for his wife being so hot on his tracks.

After a weighted silence, my thoughts evade me. "It seems that he's pissed you off, but are you sure this is the route you want to take?"

"That's really none of your concern, now is it?" Quinn refutes.

"Well, since you're eager to hire me for my services, it is my concern. You said you'd make it worth my while, but so far, I'm not impressed, especially not with bad attitudes. He's not the first or last person to cheat. If you're unhappy, then leave him. I'm not interested in getting involved with domestic disputes," I say.

I carefully place my cocktail down and rise from my chair, preparing to leave. Just as I was about to depart, eager to put this ridiculous encounter behind me, my eyes locked with hers. In them, I see the deep sea of pain in her crystal blue eyes.

She sighs. "If only it were that simple."

I sit back down, crossing my arms in front of my chest. "I'm listening."

"He's not the man I thought he was," she says.

"Most men aren't." I take another sip of my dirty martini.

I listen intently as Quinn shares the suffocating prenup and strict conditions of her marriage. I'll admit, this woman got the short end of the stick. The typical story, if you ask me, women falling in love with a rich douche and putting all her dreams and hopes into him, neglecting to be smart and protecting her rights. Her only card to play is the infidelity clause that she fought tooth and nail to have included.

She continues, "The only way to get what is rightfully mine is if he is caught red-handed. Photos of him merely talking to a woman is not enough."

"Which is why you need my help," I verify.

She sips her cocktail. "Precisely, I've thought long and hard about this. I saw the way he was looking at you. You're the woman that can help me get out of my shitty marriage."

I watch her carefully for a moment, contemplating her proposal. My eyes settle on her hand, a colossal-sized diamond staring back at me.

Finally, I say, "I can help, but it's going to cost you."

Quinn nods with eagerness. "Name your price."

I pick up my cocktail and finish it off in one long sip and then say, "One hundred thousand dollars."

THE TERMS OF OUR ARRANGEMENT WERE SIMPLE: SET THE TRAP, gather evidence, and collect the payoff. So, over the last few weeks, I got better acquainted with Clay, seducing him, drawing him into my web, and milking him for all that I could. He wined and dined me, offering me the world on a silver platter and appeasing my financial desires. I played my part, indulging in his lavish gestures while discreetly reporting our liaisons to his wife. With each calculated rendezvous, I cemented his downfall, leaving him ensnared in a trap of his own making.

Now, as Quinn approaches, a black purse clutched tightly in her hand, I wait with anticipation, her steps cautious yet purposeful. She's holding it as if the weight of its contents promises to alter the course of her calculated destiny. Our secret arrangement is poised to reshape her future. She opens the passenger car door and slides in with ease.

Seated beside me in the dim glow of the car's interior, I can sense the weight of her expectations bearing down upon her. I'd insisted that I receive at least half of my payment before completing the task. And she agreed, understanding this exchange is more than a mere transaction; it's a lifeline, one step closer for her to reclaim control over her life.

Her long fingers tap against the bag, "So, when's the next time you're meeting my husband?"

"Tonight," I say.

Her face remains stoic, "How do you plan on doing it, exactly?"

"I have my ways," I reply.

Quinn rolls her eyes, clearly unamused by my obscurity. Then she reaches into her jacket, pulling out a small vial containing a powdered white substance.

My brow perches. "What's that?"

"This is how you're going to get the photos," she answers.

"Why would I need that?" I challenge.

"My husband is a high-functioning alcoholic. I'm almost certain the cocktails he will consume won't be enough to knock him out, so you can capture what I need without any issues. This will help you get him vulnerable," she explains.

She passes it to me, and I hold it up between my thumb and index finger, carefully inspecting its contents. Little did she know, I was quite familiar with the act of drugging my sexual conquests as a means to gain better access to their wealth. But she didn't need to know that. I'd be a fool to show all the cards I have to play. After all, it's all a game, isn't it? In my world, you either play or get played. The latter has never been my MO.

I keep my thoughts to myself and place the vial into my bosom, "Is that the money?"

Quinn reaches into her bag again, pulls out a cream envelope, and hands it to me. I quickly count the cash to ensure it's what we agreed upon. Once I do, I quickly toss the envelope into my bag.

"Remember, you'll get the other half once it's done," she says.

I nod, "Sounds like a deal to me."

My phone goes off. It's a text from Clay. My eyes quickly lock with hers; the silence is stiff and awkward.

Then she half-heartedly grins, "Is that my loving husband?"

I nod and say, "Yes."

"Well, you better get to work," she says before she gets out of the vehicle, slides into her own, and drives off into the darkness.

LATER THAT NIGHT, I ZIP UP AN OXBLOOD LATEX DRESS AND reach for my favorite diamond earrings. I settle in front of my full-length mirror, giving myself a final once-over before slipping on my stilettos. I reach for my trench coat in the same deep burgundy hue and put it on, then grab my favorite designer bag. Before departing, I rummage through my apartment in search of my keys, completely ignoring the vial of drugs Quinn had given to me a little while earlier.

Fifteen minutes later, I arrive at the designated meeting spot, my heart racing with anticipation as I await Clay's arrival. The moon casts an eerie glow over the deserted street, adding to the sense of intrigue that permeates the atmosphere.

Moments pass before Clay's sleek car pulls up beside mine, the sound of its engine cutting through the silence of the night. He steps out, dressed impeccably in a tailored suit that accentuates his stature and powerful presence.

"Ready, beautiful?" he asks, a mischievous glint in his eyes as he opens my car door and offers me his arm.

I nod, a thrill coursing through me. With a confident smile, I link my arm with his, ready to immerse myself in our night ahead. He escorts me into a hidden speakeasy, tactfully disguised as a mom-and-pop style laundromat. Inside, dark green leather booths, vintage wallpaper, a charming jukebox, and decadent chandeliers fill the private bar.

Clay helps me out of my coat. "You look stunning tonight, absolutely breathtaking."

"Thank you, Clay. You're not looking too bad yourself," I say with a hinted blush.

"Just trying to keep up with you, darling." He grins.

I wink, matching his flirtation. "Smooth talker."

As the evening unfolds, Clay and I find ourselves drawn to each other with an irresistible pull. Our shared laughter and easy conversation create an undeniable chemistry, igniting a spark that lingers in the air between us.

After finishing our second round of drinks, he leans forward with a playful glint in his eyes. "There's this hotel bar you have to check out. They make the best martinis in town," he offers.

I'm certain this is his way of finally getting me to bed. Luckily for him, I'd be making sure of that one way or another.

I smile. "Lead the way."

The anticipation builds as we leave our cars parked and make our way just around the corner to the hotel. Once we reach our destination, we find the hotel bar and order a round of cocktails before sitting on the empty bar stools. Together, we watch as the bartender expertly prepares our orders and presents them to us as Clay slides over his black card. We hold up our drinks, toasting the possibilities ahead.

"Cheers," I say.

We tap our glasses, and he takes a long sip of his scotch as I drink my martini. He was right; these are indeed delicious. As we sit, I allow his hand to caress and trail up the outer parts of my thigh. I try my best to keep his attention focused there as I reach my hand out. My fingers casually brush over the pockets of his suit to see if I can feel anything worth taking. When I don't, I decide it's time to cut to the chase.

I whisper into his ear with a kiss as soft and sensual as the night breeze. "How about we get a room?"

He smiles, pleased with my proposal. "Absolutely. Why don't you wait here while I get everything situated?"

"Don't make me wait too long," I say.

He winks before heading to the receptionist with a new sense of eagerness in his step. While he's away, I order another round of drinks and instruct the bartender to put it on his tab. I carefully watch Clay pull out his credit card once more and pay for the room. Once I receive our drinks, my eyes quickly scan the room to ensure that no one is looking. When the coast is clear, I discreetly place a few sprinkles of my powdered substance into his drink and stir with a straw. I patiently wait for the contents to evaporate into the liquid before grabbing our drinks and making my way over to him in the lobby.

On our way to the room, we toast once more, and I watch as he carelessly sips his cocktail as we walk to our destination. Inside the room, the space is dimly lit, and the atmosphere crackles with a blend of desire and anticipation. Clay's touch is electric as he pulls me close, his lips leaving a path of fire along my skin. I playfully push him down onto the bed and start to dance seductively as I watch him finish off his drink.

"I want you so badly right now," he confesses.

"Then take me," I challenge.

Without saying another word, I approach him, further drawing him into my enticing web. Reaching for his hand, I place it on my breast, granting him access to my body. He leans up, trailing kisses down my neck, then to my breasts, before sliding his hands up my dress and touching my sweet spot.

"God, you're fucking hot," he says once more.

I want to roll my eyes, but I stay in character. "How bad do you want to fuck me, baby?"

He breathes, "So bad, my cock is ready to blast off."

"I want you to. But I need you to do a favor first," I say.

"What's that baby?" Clay murmurs.

"I want you to fuck me long and hard," I say.

His eyes light up at the sound of my request, "I can surely do that."

"And I want to record you fucking me," I say, looking deep into his eyes.

I can instantly sense his apprehension, but before he can dispute my request, I pull up my dress and touch myself.

"I've been imagining you fucking me since the day we met Clay. I've wanted you so bad this whole time. Touching myself thinking about you. I want to be able to relive this moment whenever I want," I say as my fingers delicately press against my flower.

By now, I'm dripping wet, my fingers covered in my honey glaze. He's completely mesmerized as I deliberately take my fingers and place them into his mouth, letting him taste me.

I watch as he slowly licks his lips, swirling my essence across his mouth. "Okay," he says.

My lips part with a smile as I reach for my bag, expertly setting up my camera to capture evidence of our encounter on the dresser. Once I'm done, I walk back over to Clay and have him stand up to join me. As I do, his eyes fixate on the camera, and I can tell he's nervous. I gently pull on his face, bringing his attention back to me.

"Let's put on a show," I say before pulling his lips to mine.

With each kiss, the heat between us intensifies, passion igniting like wildfire. Clothes are shed in a frenzy. The air is thick with the scent of arousal as we flirt with the desire to take things a step further.

I straddle him on the bed, allowing his hands to pull on and caress my breasts and ass as I sit on top of his face. He works his tongue like a true professional, licking and sucking on my womanhood until I climax. Pleased, I kiss him once more, and I grind my hips into his stiffness. He is more than ready. I watch as he reaches for a condom inside his wallet. When he retrieves it, I help him guide it on, expertly stroking his member and tracing my tongue around the nape of his neck. Suddenly, I can see his eyelids grow heavy, a sure indication that my special recipe is working its magic. Then, without warning, I feel his body go slightly limp. His chest gently rises and falls as he drifts into a deep, sedated sleep.

Beside him, his recently discarded wallet captures my attention. I reach for it, pulling out the few hundred-dollar bills neatly folded up inside. Content, I place the money into my purse and dismount from his body. Without hesitation, I quietly slip on my dress, gather my belongings, and glide out of the hotel without drawing attention to myself. I step out into the darkness and hurry into my ride, seemingly unseen. Once inside my car, I send a text to Quinn.

Me:

It's done.

Pleased, I pull off into the night and head home.

CHAPTER

Three

EMERGING FROM THE SHADOWS

Tempest

The twisted woman looking back at me looks poised, elegant, even. Yet, her demeanor is pained, her secrets buried in the deepest and darkest depths of her eyes. Disappointment fills her pupils, fear intertwines with her lashes, and her eyelids are coated in sadness. These peculiar, bicolored eyes seemingly burn into my soul, leaving me in a trance.

"What brings you in today, Tempest?" my therapist, Dr. Jacqueline Nelson, says, warping me back into reality.

"Is this new?" I ask, pointing toward the painting in front of me.

Despite countless visits over the last five months, the disjointed woman on the canvas stands out like a sore thumb.

Dr. Nelson smiles and tilts her head slightly, looking over her shoulder. "The Portrait of Dora Maar. Are you familiar with Picasso?"

I nod. "Briefly in high school, I guess."

"Some would say that he was one of the most legendary artists of his time," she responds.

"I thought you could only see his stuff in art museums or something like that," I admit. My eyes quickly take stock of her perfectly manicured nails, fancy decor, and affluent aura, "You must do very well for yourself," I say.

She chuckles. "While I'm flattered by your assumption, this is a replica. One of these could easily go for millions of dollars."

My eyes expand with astonishment, "Millions? That's insane. Who in their right mind would pay millions of dollars for something like that?"

A grin covers Dr. Nelson's face once more. "I take it you're not a fan."

My gaze fixates on the woman's eyes once more. I strain to see beyond what meets the eye but am unable to get past its oddities. In fact, the more that I look at the woman, the more disconcerted I become. I can feel Dr. Nelson studying my movements. I wonder if she will make note of this.

Shifting in my seat, I say, "It's not that, per se. It's just that I don't understand it. And her eyes are kind of making me feel uncomfortable."

This time, she uses her swivel chair to turn around completely, facing the object of my discontent.

For a moment, she studies the painting with me, then says, "Isn't that the beauty of art? It evokes diverse feelings, and all interpretations are subjective."

I shrug, knowing the only other time I'd given this much attention to art or anything remotely close was during class field trips to the Art Museum. But I say, "Sure, I guess. What do you see when you look at it?"

She turns back to face me now, giving me her full attention, "I see a very beautiful woman who is sad. She's battling an imbalance within herself, trying to fit into societal expectations yet attempting to stay true to the essence of her being. Which is not an easy feat, especially during that time. History has shown that it has never been easy to be a woman, wouldn't you agree?"

I nod, completely amazed by her expert assessment. "Actually, I do."

Dr. Nelson smiles again. "Well, Tempest, as much as I'd love to sit and talk about the workings of Picasso and the many complexities of art, you called wanting a last-minute session with me. Is everything all right? You sounded very distressed over the phone."

I nervously chew on my bottom lip. She's right. I am distracting myself.

She can sense my apprehension. "Are you nervous about returning to work today?"

I nod, allowing my palms to grip the edge of the upholstered couch. After everything I've been through, especially recently, I desperately need some truth and clarity. I've come a long way since I started seeing Dr. Nelson. With her encouragement, I now understand that I can no longer live in the shadows and hide from the responsibilities of my life. After taking a ten-month leave from work, checking myself into a rehabilitation facility, and staying committed to my therapy sessions twice a week, I finally built up enough courage to return to life as I once knew it. It took a lot of deep work and commitment to claw my way out of the darkness I've lived in for so long. But I know that this is just the tip of the iceberg. The work of healing is far from done.

Although my parents left me an inheritance, those funds covered college and allowed me to build a pretty comfortable life for myself without stressing much about money. Even with some medical bills, I've managed to maintain a modest life-style, so I wasn't in dire need of going back to work. I simply could no longer avoid certain aspects of my life. I felt ready—at least, that's what I initially thought. But now, I'm not so sure.

At first, I was eager to get back into the swing of things. But as the weeks dwindled down to days and then hours, an all-consuming sense of dread gripped me like invisible shack-les, making it hard to breathe. I had a full-blown panic attack, forcing me to second-guess all the progress I thought I'd made. Deep down, I'm terrified this might be a huge mistake. I'm not sure I'm ready—or if I ever will be.

"How about you walk me through what you're feeling?" Dr. Nelson asks, leaning back into her chair.

"I'm nervous. I'm not sure if I'm ready, to be honest. What if I fall off the rails again?"

The anxiety and depression just got to be too much to bear. I never want to return to that space in my life, ever.

Her eyes are empathetic. "I can't guarantee that you won't."

The bluntness of her statement stings.

She continues, "What's important and different from be-fore is that you have the tools to manage those tough feelings when they arise. The road to recovery after battling addiction and overcoming trauma is not linear. I can't say that you won't face temptation because you may, and you likely will make mistakes. What's important is to be patient and gracious with yourself and your healing during this time. As long as you stay committed, your mental health will evolve and grow stronger. But it's vital to remember that you have no control over the world outside of you. The only thing you have dominion over is yourself and your choice to stay the course. Eventually, the efforts you employ to create a healthy lifestyle for yourself will come to be as easy as breathing."

"How am I supposed to do that in my line of work? There are emotional triggers everywhere that I turn," I ask, dumbfounded.

"For starters, you can't keep your feelings bottled up inside of you. Compartmentalize, yes, but don't harbor those thoughts or emotions. They will only compound and fester until they erupt in the most inconvenient way possible," she explains.

"Like last time," I mumble.

The memories of my downward spiral are still vividly clear in my mind.

"We've never discussed this before, but why did you choose to become a cop?" Dr. Nelson asks, interrupting my thoughts.

The question, although seemingly simple, feels loaded. Had I known then what I know now, I'm not sure I would have chosen this life for myself. It's never been easy being caught between the two worlds of Black and Blue.

My mind carefully considers my response, and then I reply, "I wanted to help people, especially those who look like me. I figured it would be more advantageous to work from the other side and try to make progress that way."

"That's very honorable, Tempest. Do you feel like you've been able to help others?"

I ponder over her question for a moment, unsure of how to answer. A few paused seconds pass before I slowly nod my head yes. My hesitation to answer served as a reflection of my personal plight.

If I am being honest, it has been one of the most challenging realities I've endured. Through it all, I have helped others and brought forth justice. My nearly perfect case closure rate would support that claim. But deep down, I wonder if my quest to help others resulted in me hurting myself. I've never felt that I quite fit in anywhere or that my dedication and hard work were appreciated. Instead, I faced distrust from the community, scrutiny from my peers, and passive disregard from my colleagues. Carrying the weight of it all has been exhausting.

She looks at me with softness in her eyes. "That's amazing and something to be very proud of. Just remember, if you practice self-awareness and healthy ways to release, you will be fine. I have faith in you, Tempest. You should try having some faith in yourself."

I take a deep breath, forcing myself to heed her words.

"You're right," I say, trying to convince myself.

She nods. "And when you feel like it's too much, I will be here to support you for as long as you need. I am only one phone call away."

"What about text, email?" I smirk, a canny attempt to lighten the mood.

"That too," Dr. Nelson says with a warm gaze.

I let out an exasperated sigh and rise out of my seat. "Thank you for fitting me in this morning. I know that you're busy."

She stands from her chair and leads me to the door before turning to wink at me. "The pleasure is all mine."

As I step out of her office and walk through the waiting room, I keep my head down, hoping to avoid glances from her other patient, whose session I'm sure to have interrupted with my sudden and desperate request.

Once on the elevator, I check my watch. I had about an hour before I had to report to work, plenty of time to stop by my favorite café, Peddler Coffee, just around the corner. A few seconds pass, and I step off the elevator and out into the busy morning. I dig my hands in my pockets, enduring the brutal morning chill, and take a short walk there.

Brown sugar and vanilla latte in hand, I trek to my car, ready to start my day and get back to reality. Once I'm inside, I use my keys to start the engine of my Lexus. As I wait for it to warm up, I turn on a playlist filled with positive affirmations sent to me by Dr. Nelson.

Closing my eyes, I repeat the words back to myself, "I am capable. I am worthy. I am powerful."

I do this for a few minutes before deeply inhaling and exhaling, breath work that I learned in rehab. Moments later, I take one last deep breath and then shift my car into drive, pulling off into the morning traffic and joining the mindless flow of society once again.

THE BUILDING HOUSING THE NINTH POLICE DISTRICT LOOKS old and weathered, its faded brick facade and cracked windowsills telling stories of countless years of service. I clutch onto my briefcase for dear life, making my best attempt to look poised and in control. But as I draw closer to the building's entrance, my body tenses.

Once I approach the door, I take another calming breath and pull on the cold handle before stepping inside. I walk past the security desk using my badge to gain entry. When I do, my pulse quickens, waiting for my access to be granted. Milliseconds feel like hours, and then, when I see the tiny light turn from red to green, relief washes over me.

I proceed toward the elevators, pressing the call button to go up. A few moments later, the doors open, and a group of street patrolmen step off. I see a few familiar faces. A reflection of the city's struggles to attract and recruit new hires to join the good fight. All but one ignores me as if I'm not even there—something I've grown quite accustomed to during my time here. We lock eyes, and he greets me with a welcoming nod. I return his gesture before stepping onto the old elevator and riding up quietly with my thoughts.

Within seconds, the elevator bell softly rings, indicating my arrival or impending doom. When I step off, I'm instantly greeted by the sound of rustling papers, phones ringing, and fingers frantically typing against keyboards. Head down, I make my way toward my old desk unnoticed. I'm pleased when I see it in the distance, eager to finally find reprieve in something familiar.

At my desk, I peel off my coat and shove my work bag into the drawer before pulling my chair out to take a seat. I stare at my workstation, taking it all in, my computer, accolades, and pictures still in their dutiful spots.

"Hi, Detective Blaze?" an unfamiliar voice speaks from behind me.

I turn to see another woman standing there. She's petite, yet fit. Her thick hair is pulled back into a sleek bun, showcasing the honey glow and rich warmth of her innocent face. The aura of her fresh enthusiasm radiates. She's clearly a D1.

I reply, "Yes."

She smiles. "It's so nice to meet you, I'm Maldonado, Emma Maldonado. But my friends and family call me Em."

Maldonado extends her hand, offering a handshake. I reach out and return the gesture.

"I just started a few weeks ago. I used to be on street patrol until I got moved to this unit," she continues.

I watch as she takes a seat at the desk next to mine. "How do you like it?"

Maldonado shrugs. "Honestly, it's been pretty slow. All they have me doing is logging evidence and screening their calls. But I guess we've all got to start somewhere."

I can almost immediately sense the curiosity and eagerness for the job that I once had.

"Very true," I say.

"I hope that you don't mind. I took the liberty of cleaning up around your desk. It was collecting a bit of dust," she confesses.

"Not at all. That was very nice of you. Thank you." I grin.

"Blaze!" is called out in the background, interrupting our friendly banter.

I look over my shoulder and see Sergeant Sterling's head peeking out of his office door. If I managed to quietly blend in before, all that has now vanished as all eyes are on me. He raises his hand in the air, waving for me to come in. I nervously tuck my hair behind my ear and rise from my chair. Maldonado locks eyes with mine, giving me an encouraging wink before I make my way back toward his office.

My heart races with each step that I take. As I do, I silently repeat the affirmations in my head and keep my composure. Once I reach his doorway, Sterling is glued to his computer screen, a look of frustration filling his eyes. His desk is hidden under a sea of file folders, papers, and old coffee cups. He barely looks up to acknowledge my presence, but he uses his free hand to motion for me to close the door and sit down.

I do as I'm told, closing the door and sitting down in the chair positioned in front of his desk. "Sir," I say.

I watch silently as he furiously types on his keyboard. Once he's done, he places his elbows on the desk, weaving his fingers together under his chin. "How are you feeling, Blaze?" he asks.

"I'm good, sir. Ready to get back out there."

Sergeant Sterling finally shows some semblance of gratitude for my return. He was very understanding of my time away. It was a small gesture that I greatly appreciated, and I wanted to ensure he did not regret advocating for my return.

"Good, good," he says, his words laced with relief. "We've been drowning without you," he confesses.

I nod once more.

"I can use all the help I can get around here. The city is crawling with criminals, we're swimming in a shitload of bodies, and the mayor is not happy, especially with a reelection year right around the corner."

"Absolutely, sir. I've been keeping up with the news," I reply.

He continues, "I'm not sending you out to the field just yet, but I am going to need your help reviewing these reports. No one seems to have your eye."

He reaches for a stack of folders on his desk, placing my badge on top of the pile before handing the items to me, "See if you can make sense of any of this shit."

"Yes, sir," I say before rising out of my seat and grabbing them.

Back at my desk, I crack open my laptop and use my old credentials to log in, eager to dive in. While I wait for it to power up, I sift through the piles of folders. As I do, I feel a familiar sense of adrenaline course through my veins. But after about an hour, I rub my temples, the details of each unsolved case swirling in my head. Sterling was right. The department is up to their ass in cases. This was not going to be an easy feat.

One report in particular catches my eye. I type the case number into the system and read through the details of the record. I stare at the pictures of Karina Allegro. She'd been found naked, dismembered, and drained of her blood. There were no witnesses, no clues, and seemingly, no leads.

"Blaze, is that you? We must really be in a heap of trouble if they let you back," a familiar voice comes from over my shoulder, causing my skin to crawl.

I look up and see Detective McGregor, the next in line for sergeant, I'm sure, and a piping asshole. It's apparent that not much has changed during my time away. For he's still the same condescending and tone-deaf asshole he was back then.

McGregor continues, "It's a wonder they didn't stick you on desk duty where you belong, you know, since you're so fragile."

I ignore him, keeping my cool. I knew he was counting on me to lash out simply to reaffirm his beliefs about the 'Angry Black Woman' narrative that he and so many others readily weaponize at their convenience. His laugh rings in my ears as he finally walks away and toward his desk.

"Pendejo," Maldonado mutters under her breath.

I swallow my irritation and rise from my seat, "Will you excuse me for a moment?"

She nods, her eyes empathetic. I quickly make my way to the bathroom. As I step out into the corridor, my skin is hot and burning with rage. I'm angry, that's for damn sure. I keep toward my destination, anxious for reprieve. Once I reach it, I walk to the sink and furiously turn on the faucets. Cool water coats my hands as I rub them together. A few moments pass as I gather myself, using my wet fingertips to touch the nape of my neck.

I lean my hands against the sink and tap my foot, taking a few deep, calming breaths and looking at the floor. Then I slowly lift my head, standing there, staring into the mirror, questioning my decision to willingly return to this.

My mahogany brown skin is smooth and creamy, my individual box braids are perfectly parted, each plait expertly weaved down my back. On the outside, I look as presentable and put-together as one can be, I guess. It's just on the inside, I feel like a complete mess.

"You got this," I whisper to myself.

I allow a few more minutes to pass before I finally regain my composure and step out into the hallway. As I pass by an old vending machine on the way back to my desk, ready to brave through it, the sudden craving for something sweet prompts me to stop in my tracks. I reach into my pants pocket, pull out a crumbled dollar bill, inserting it into the machine. After making my selection, I bend down, digging my hand into the small opening to fish out my selection before eagerly tearing off the wrappers to bite into my sweet release. Pleased, I close my eyes and enjoy the taste of my milk chocolate for a moment.

As I pass the elevator, I open my mouth to take another bite, but as I do, the doors glide open. His striking brown eyes immediately lock with mine. The shock of seeing his face sends my stomach into convulsions, causing me to drop my candy bar to the ground.

"Shit!" I say, quickly leaning down to retrieve it.

I rise, ready to bolt and hide under my cubicle, but as I do, his hand reaches out, touching mine. My body tenses at the closeness, our skin colliding. For so many nights, I longed for his touch. It was in these very halls that we first crossed paths and became entangled with one another. I was a rookie cop, and he was a newly hired lawyer with the district attorney's office. We were both so young, both so full of promise. I quickly push the memories of us out of my head.

"Tempest, wow. It's nice to see that you're back. How are you?" Lance, the former love of my life, asks.

The question almost makes me laugh. How am I? It's especially funny that he is so concerned with my state of being right now when he, in fact, left me when I needed him most.

"PLEASE DON'T DO THIS," I BEG, MY VOICE TREMBLING, THE DESPERA-tion clear in every word.

"I'm sorry, Tempest, I can't do this anymore," Lance says, his face firm, his eyes void of the warmth they once held. The finality in his tone hits me like a punch to the gut.

It's New Year's Eve. We should be celebrating. We should be sealing our future with a kiss. Instead, tears stream down my face as I struggle to keep my voice steady. "I know things have been crazy, but I can be better. I will be better. I'm not okay, Lance, I need help."

He shakes his head, my pleas seemingly falling on deaf ears. His expression doesn't soften, doesn't crack. With bags in hand, he walks toward the door of our home, the home we share, placing his hand on the doorknob. He pauses, turning to look at me one last time. "It's just all too much. I can't help you, Tempest. I'm not sure I ever could."

"I thought you loved me, Lance. You said you wanted to marry me," I cry out, my voice breaking. "What happened to 'you and I, through thick and thin'?"

His eyes, once full of love and promise, now look at me with some-thing else—pity, maybe even relief. "You haven't been you for a very long time now. Ever since…" his voice trails off.

"Don't you dare! Don't you fucking dare throw that in my face," I sneer.

He exhales deeply, choosing his next words carefully, "I'm not sure you'll ever be you again," he says, his voice calm, detached, as if he's talking to a stranger.

I stare into his eyes, searching for some semblance of hope, but my heart sinks when I see that the love he once had for me has vanished, com-pletely evaporated. The realization strikes me like a dagger to the chest.

"I know I've been struggling for a while, but that's normal, right? I will get better. Don't you believe in me? In us?" I challenge, my voice barely above a whisper, a last-ditch effort to hold on to something that's already slipping away.

Lance's jaw tightens, his usual soft cocoa brown features now hard and unyielding. "I wish you all the best, Temp. But I can't do this with you any longer." His voice is final.

I watch as the love of my life, the man I thought I'd spend forever with, walks out of my life. The door closes with a soft click, but to me, it feels like an explosion. He's gone, leaving me alone with the echoes of our broken dreams, our shattered future, and promises unkept.

Hours later, the house feels impossibly quiet after he leaves, the silence pressing in on me, suffocating me.

Me:

> Lance is gone. He left me. Now, I truly have no one.

I send the text and stare off into space. Moments later, I manage to pull myself out of the bed we shared. The memory forces me to fall to my knees, the weight of his departure crushing me once more, squeezing the air out of my lungs. My chest tightens, my breath coming in ragged gasps. I can't breathe. I can't think. All I can do is feel the overwhelming pain, the devastation that's ripping me apart from the inside out.

In a daze, I rise up and stumble toward the bathroom, my vision blurred by tears. The medicine cabinet creaks as I open it, my hands shaking uncontrollably. The bottles of pills that I've come to depend on over this last year seem to blur together, their labels indistinguishable. My heart pounds in my ears, drowning out all rational thought.

I pour a handful of pills into my palm, staring at them through the haze of my tears. Maybe this will make it stop—the pain, the heartbreak, the overwhelming sense of loss that seems to consume my life.

I swallow the pills, one by one, chasing them with a swig from a half-empty bottle of whiskey that I had hidden under the sink. The burning sensation in my throat is nothing compared to the fire raging in my chest.

As I sink to the floor, the world around me begins to fade. The pain in my chest intensifies, but it's different now—duller, more distant. I welcome the numbness as it spreads through my body, a welcome reprieve from the agony that has consumed me.

The last thing I hear before the darkness overtakes me completely is the sound of ambulance sirens in the distance, their wails growing louder, echoing in my mind like a haunting melody. But it's too late. I'm too far gone. I let the shadows claim me, pulling me under, grateful for the silence that follows.

I CAN FEEL HIS EYES ON ME AS I RECOUNT OUR LAST ENCOUNTER and all that followed. The memories flood back in vivid, painful detail—his words, his coldness, the door closing behind him. The betrayal that led me to the edge. I fight to keep my composure, swallowing down the bitterness that rises in my throat.

I finally meet his gaze head-on, staring straight into the man I once knew. His glasses are new, sleek, and polished, making him look more refined, more put-together. He seems fitter than I remember, his shoulders broader, his posture more confident, as if the weight of our past has lifted from him entirely. It infuriates me how he can stand there, looking irritatingly more handsome than I could ever recall, while I'm still struggling to piece myself back together.

But beneath the anger, there's a dull ache, a longing for what we once had. I hate that I still miss him, I still miss what we were before everything fell apart.

"I'm better now," I say, my voice steady, though it takes everything in me to keep it that way. I force the words out, each one a declaration of my strength, my survival. I won't let him see the cracks beneath the surface.

I turn on my heels and promptly walk back to my desk, clutching onto my dignity as best I can. My hands are trembling, but I keep them busy, flipping open one of the file folders and begin to type my notes. The familiar rhythm of the keys beneath my fingers grounds me, giving me something to focus on other than the whirlwind of emotions crashing inside me.

"You got this, you got this," I mutter to myself repeatedly, a mantra to keep me steady.

The words are more for me than for anyone else, a reminder that I'm still here, still fighting, still moving forward—even if it feels like I'm dragging myself through quicksand.

CHAPTER

Four

DELICATE FACADES

Stormy

Drip.

Drip.

Drip.

Small droplets fall from the faucet into the pool of water mixed with luxurious oils and scented bubbles. The heat from the bath creates a steamy haze, opening my pores. I lift my leg, using my big toe to catch the loose water pearls. Sinking deeper into the bath, I take it all in. With closed eyes, I let my body go heavy, completely relaxing and drifting into my daydreams. Moments later, my phone softly chimes. The sound interrupts my solace.

I let out a heavy sigh and rise from the tub, stretching my arm to grab the towel hanging on the door. Taking my time, I dry my body off, carefully following my skincare regimen with an assortment of lavish body butters, serums, and creams. Once finished, I slip into my plush robe and walk through my apartment, pulling my hair into a messy bun as I head to the kitchen.

At the stove, I turn the chrome knob, pausing to listen to the click as the flame ignites, heating the teapot on the front burner. I reach overhead and pull out my favorite coffee mug, a cherished gift from Ms. Gwen. As the water warms up, I move to the living room and turn on the television. I spend the next few moments surfing through the channels before settling on the morning news. In my line of work, it's advantageous to stay informed about the city's latest happenings and scandals I could possibly exploit.

Moments later, the tea kettle hisses, grabbing my attention. Back in the kitchen, I promptly turn off the stove and fix my morning tea just the way I like it, with a dash of honey and a splash of lemon juice. Walking back into my living room, I head to my grand windows and press the control on the wall panel, prompting my floor-length curtains to open. Welcoming the sunlight in, I stand there for a moment, sipping my tea and taking in the scenic view of the Center City skyline. William Penn sits atop the metropolis in the distance, watching over us all, saints and sinners alike.

Philadelphia, the city of brotherly love, or lately as I like to call it, Gotham fucking City. For all the beauty there is to get lost in, from the history, the food, the architecture, and culture, there's this undeniable dark cloud that seems to constantly loom, bringing violence, deceit, and straight-up debauchery.

I'll admit, I'm far from a saint, but I do what I must to survive, navigating the path of right and wrong as best I can.

I've managed to walk a tightrope between the two worlds for as long as I can remember. Hell, it's all I've known. With all the people I've screwed and shit that I've done, it's a wonder that I'm not dead and missing like so many others. Lord knows I've come dangerously close. The recent string of murders, claiming the lives of two of my friends, has left me on edge, to say the least. The perpetrator—a deranged killer whose mere existence has haunted me since our paths last crossed—has instilled a sense of unease that lingers in the air like a foul smell. A single chill crawls up my spine as I realize just how close I'd come to death. I can't help but wonder if I could've been her next victim.

I quickly push those thoughts out of my mind and take another sip of my tea. As each day passes, it's becoming clearer that I have to move on from this city and get out of this dangerous game once and for all. But as much as I'd like to, something keeps holding me back, like an invisible shackle that's keeping me here.

"One day," I softly say to myself.

I take a deep breath, shoving my aspirations away. After all, there's work to be done, and sacrifices must be made. I've come too far to turn back now. In times like these, one would be foolish not to capitalize on the shifting currents of fate, and I'm no fool. As bodies continue to pile up and the city descends further into turmoil, I find myself navigating a treacherous landscape where survival depends on one's ability to seize every opportunity that presents itself.

I spend the next hour sorting through the footage of Clay and my encounter, careful to edit out any incriminating evidence. Pleased, I reach my hands above my head to stretch. Just then, my phone rings, pulling me out of my trance. I set my tea down on a coaster, and pick up my cell.

Quinn:

Tomorrow. 2 p.m. at the old distillery on Lee Street.

Me:

I'll be there.

Pleased, I take another sip of my tea, eager to receive the rest of my payment. My phone rings again. This time, it is a text from one of my sponsors.

Mark:

I did something bad, and I need to be punished.

Before I can reply, a notification of five thousand dollars being deposited into my account comes through. I smile at the promise of more cash coming my way. Nothing turns me on more than the power of the dollar.

LATER THAT DAY, THE ROOM IS DIMLY LIT, JUST THE WAY I LIKE IT. A single lamp in the corner casts long shadows across the walls, accentuating the rich, deep red hues of the decor. The air is thick with the scent of leather and a subtle hint of sandalwood, a fragrance that clings to the expensive furnishings like a secret.

I stand in the center of the room, dressed in a black leather catsuit, the material hugging my curves like a second skin. My heels click against the hardwood floor as I take a step forward, each movement deliberate and calculated. I know that

Mark is watching me, his eyes following my every move. He won't dare speak unless I tell him to. He knows better.

As soon as Mark arrived in the city from Miami, he insisted that I meet him at his Philadelphia penthouse, more specifically, the hidden room he's converted into his personal sex dungeon, to play.

Now he's kneeling in the center of the room, his head bowed, hands tied, waiting patiently for my command. The soft light catches the lines of his body, highlighting the tension in his muscles, the anticipation that radiates off him in waves. He's in his element here, a place where he can temporarily discard the mask he wears and let his innate nature shine through. On the surface, he's a prominent and well-respected angel investor, but deep down, Mark has darker desires. In this room, his successes and riches don't mean a thing. This is our ritual—our unspoken agreement, where I take the reins, and he completely surrenders.

Against one wall stands a large, deep crimson velvet chaise lounge, the kind that invites you to sink into it and never leave. Beside it, a small table holds an array of items—silk ropes, leather cuffs, nipple clamps, and various other tools of the trade, all neatly arranged and ready for use. I walk up to the table and let my hands lightly brush over the toys before settling on a delicately crafted flogger. Its relative thickness and leather tail would surely give the perfect mixture of pleasure and pain. He may have all the money in the world, but in here, in this room, he's mine to shape, to mold, and to control.

"Look at me," I command, my voice low, authoritative.

Mark lifts his head, his eyes meeting mine, wide and expectant. There's a fire behind them, a burning desire that's both desperate and eager. He needs to please me, to obey.

"Good boy," I purr, walking around him in a slow circle, my whip trailing lightly across his shoulders and his back.

I stop in front of him, reaching out to lift his chin with my finger, forcing him to look up at me.

"So, you've been a bad boy? You know what that means, don't you?" I ask, already knowing the answer.

"Yes, Mistress," he replies, his voice barely above a whisper, full of reverence.

I can see the faint tremble in his muscles, the tension in his posture as he waits for my next move.

"You'll take whatever I give you, won't you?" I ask, and he nods again, more vigorously this time.

"Yes, Mistress," he breathes, his voice trembling with a mix of fear and desire.

I strike him lightly with the whip, watching as his body tenses, a sharp gasp escaping his lips. I do it again, slightly harder this time, and he groans, his back arching. I can see the conflict in his body—the pleasure and pain mingling together, and it excites me.

"That's it," I purr, striking him once more, leaving a faint red line across his ass. "Take it all for me."

An hour later, I murmur, "You did well," pressing a soft kiss to his forehead as he lies there, still catching his breath.

Mark collapses onto the bed, spent and satisfied, his chest heaving as he struggles to catch his breath. I stand, watching him, the remnants of our session still buzzing through the air like static electricity. His body, once tense with anticipation, now lies in a state of complete surrender, every muscle relaxed, every nerve thoroughly spent.

I take my time, slowly untying the knots that bind his wrists, letting the silk rope slip free from his skin. The marks will fade, but the memory of our time together will linger—just the way he likes it. He looks up at me, a lazy smile curving his lips, the kind of smile that speaks of contentment.

"That was… incredible," he murmurs, his voice hoarse, laced with lingering pleasure.

I offer him a small, satisfied smile, enjoying the sight of him in this state—completely at my mercy and loving every second of it.

"I know," I reply, my voice cool and controlled, the power dynamic between us still very much in place.

Mark sits up slowly, running a hand through his tousled hair, his breathing gradually returning to normal, "Are you doing anything fun tomorrow for Halloween?" he asks, his tone casual, but there's an undercurrent of something more—an invitation, perhaps. "I got invited to this private party, and I heard things get pretty wild. We could have some serious fun."

I raise an eyebrow, intrigued but not showing it. "What kind of party?"

A playful gleam coats his eyes. "Super exclusive, no-holds-barred. You know the kind." His lips curl into a smirk, as if he's dangling a tempting offer in front of me, waiting to see if I'll bite.

I cross my arms, considering his words. I've been to parties like that before—places where the rules don't apply, where desires are indulged, and where the night can take you to the brink of pleasure and beyond. With everyone's senses blurred and good judgment cast aside, it'll surely make for an easy way to make some quick cash.

"What time?" I ask, my voice calm, betraying none of the curiosity that's beginning to bubble beneath the surface.

"Starts at ten," he says, a hint of eagerness in his tone. "I'll text you the details. It'll be worth your while, trust me."

I let a small smile play at the corners of my lips. "We'll see," I reply, leaving the decision hanging in the air, just out of reach.

THE NEXT DAY, STORM CLOUDS GATHER OMINOUSLY OVERHEAD. I make my way through the foggy streets and to our designated meeting spot. I quickly check the bag to my side, which holds the evidence Quinn is seeking.

Upon arrival, I park my car, grab my bag, and step out onto the street. The abandoned warehouse is decorated with colorful works of graffiti and broken glass. When I walk inside, the air is heavy with the rich aroma of aged spirits mingling with the musty scent of weathered wood. The vast space is poorly lit, the only light filtering in through dusty windows high above. Rows upon rows of towering oak barrels line the walls, their weathered surfaces adorned with intricate patterns of moisture stains and age-old labels, each one a testament to the passage of time and the craft of distillation. In the distance, Quinn's silhouette emerges from the shadows. I approach cautiously, my instincts on full alert.

"Did you bring them?" she says, her voice tense, betraying her nervousness.

I shrug. "Depends. Do you have my money?"

She rolls her eyes but reaches down into the black leather tote she brought along. I

carefully watch as she opens it, pulling out an envelope much like the last one. She counts out fifty thousand dollars in crisp, hundred-dollar bills, handing them over to me with a mixture of resignation and gratitude.

"Here," Quinn says, her voice laced with bitterness.

I accept the cash without uttering a word, tucking it away safely in my bag. Glancing at Quinn, I can see the exhaustion etched into her face, the weight of her secrets heavy upon her shoulders. Pleased, I pull out the thumb drive. She holds her hand out as I place it into her palm.

She quickly retrieves her laptop, inserting the drive into the USB port. I watch, waiting for a grimace or some type of emotion as she scans through the pictures and evidence of me fucking her husband. But to my surprise, there's nothing.

"They're perfect," Quinn breathes, a sense of satisfaction creeping into her voice. "Exactly what I needed."

"Glad you think so," I mutter.

She swiftly removes the drive from her computer and dumps it into her purse.

"Do me a favor," she says.

"What's that?" I ask.

"Forget you ever met me." Without saying another word, Quinn steps out into the now pouring rain, leaving me to my own devices.

I snort to myself. "Bitch."

As the rain continues to fall, I turn to leave, the echoes of our transaction fading into the stormy day.

THAT NIGHT, I ADJUST MY MASK, A STUNNING VENETIAN CRE-ation I snagged from a costume shop on South Street. Swarovski crystals adorn the black satin, tracing delicate patterns across my nose and cheekbones, leaving only my slender jawline and full, pillowy lips exposed to the night. Peering out the window, I relish the opportunity to immerse myself in the revelry of the evening. Halloween, with its promise of mischief and mayhem, has always held a special allure for me. It's a night where inhibitions are shed, and one's shadow comes alive.

Turns out, Mark got pulled away for some kind of urgent business matter and had to head back to Miami. Which is fine by me—I prefer to be alone at these types of engagements anyway.

As I approach my destination, I see an enormous brass gate, its large pillars wrapping around the entire property. Tall light posts and trees blanket the estate, while the front entrance is manned by three armed guards wearing gold-plated masks.

A valet attendant greets me as I put my car into park. I take his hand to aid my exit, and the crisp night air greets my skin. After an unseasonably hot summer, autumn appears to finally be upon us. I tug on the hood of my ruby-red cape before making my way to the entrance.

Moments later, a petite woman donning a golden peacock mask decorated with elegant blue and bronze feathers greets me. The matching jacket of her metallic gold-colored suit does little to cover her bare breasts.

She smiles, an electronic tablet in hand. "Password?"

"Lascivious," I reply, careful to follow all of Mark's instructions in order to gain entry.

"Welcome to Désir Sauvage. Are you aware of the rules?" she says.

I nod my head. "Yes, no phones."

"Would you mind if security checked you out?" she asks.

"Not at all," I reply.

Without hesitation, I spread my hands out, forming the letter "T" with my arms. As I do, one of the guards uses a metal detector to scan over my body. Leaving my gun in the car wasn't ideal, but I didn't want to risk drawing too much attention to myself upon entering. When the guard's inspection is done, the hostess smiles and then waves her hand, signaling me to follow her inside.

Upon walking into the house, we stop in a large vestibule, and she turns to me. "Please leave your belongings here."

Makeshift lockers line the walls, and she opens a free one, prompting me to follow suit. Without protest, I place my phone into it and lock it up. I can feel her eyes scanning every inch of my body as I do. I know that my choice of a sexy rendition of Little Red Riding Hood, complimented by a black skintight lace bodysuit that perfectly displays every curvature of my body, was a good choice. Paired with my trusty "Come fuck me" boots, I was confident that I'd have my way tonight. After I shut the locker, looping the key band around my wrist, the hostess signals for me to follow her once more. I oblige her, following as she leads me toward large double doors that are as high as the ceiling.

When she reaches them, she turns to me, smiling once more. She then places her index finger to her mouth and makes a "Shh" gesture with her lips.

"Have fun," she says before nodding her head and excusing herself.

I can still hear the echo of the hostess's heels trekking against the grand marble floors as she disappears through the foyer. When I push open the doors, a wave of cigar and weed smoke greets me, swirling in the dimly lit room illuminated by neon blue strobe lights. The atmosphere crackles with mischievous energy, igniting my senses with a heady mix of lust, power, and decadence. People mingle in various states of drinking, talking, dancing, and engaging in intimate encounters, their uninhibited antics a testament to the hedonistic spirit of the night.

I navigate through the space, my eyes scanning the crowd as I soak in the pulsating rhythm of the music. Moments later, I step out into the corridor, the golden plaque reading 'The Sapphire Room' serving as a marker of my location. Intrigued by the faint sounds from nearby, I follow the music to 'The Ruby Room.'

Inside, an Olympic-sized pool takes center stage, its crimson waters sprinkled with naked bodies engaged in uninhibited lust. Men lounging on chairs indulge in cigars and cognac, their conversation a backdrop to the sensual spectacle unfolding before them. I make my way to the bar, ordering a glass of champagne as I survey the scene with a discerning eye.

Sipping my drink, I observe the captivating display before me, searching for someone who catches my interest. However, none seem to meet my standards, so I finish my champagne and decide to move on.

Stepping back into the hallway, I'm drawn to a grand staircase ahead, its steps crowded with a mixture of guests. As I navigate through the horde, I catch glimpses of intimate encounters unraveling around me. An older man ensnared by the lure of two beautiful women, sex workers, I presume, bidding me to join.

As tempting as the invitation may be, I smile and lean in very close to his ear, "I don't like sharing."

Unbeknownst to him, I casually slip my hand into his pant pocket, pulling out a wad of cash secured with a clip. I discreetly slide the money into the thigh of my boot and proceed on my way. With a subtle nod to the silver fox and his companions, I continue my exploration through the rest of the lavish party.

At the top of the steps, I count five entryways lining the corridor. As I do, my eyes scan the corners of the ceilings, half-expecting to find hidden cameras. Surprisingly, none are in sight, which only means that some serious shit must go down here, shit that they want to keep hidden.

At the end of the hallway, two rooms flank me, 'The Emerald Room' stands to my left, while 'The Amethyst Room' stands to the right. Opting for the 'The Amethyst Room,' I'm instantly enveloped by opulence once I step inside. Purple and gold drapes adorn the walls, crystal chandeliers casting a decadent glow. In the center of the room, an orgy unfolds, a full spectacle of flesh and desire. I slip through the space, my masterful fingers snatching valuables from unsuspecting pockets before stepping back into the hallway.

In 'The Emerald Room,' I glide through the crowd like a shadow, my senses attuned to every opportunity that presents itself. As I flirt and seduce, my hands move skillfully, sliding into pockets and purses with practiced precision. Each stolen item adds to the thrill of the night. As I work the room, spotting a few familiar faces along the way. One is a district judge, and the other, a professional basketball player.

Back inside the corridor, the music from the party fades, replaced by an eerie silence. Ahead, two feminine figures glide through the corridor, their faces obscured by shimmering gold masks and black capes flowing behind them. Something about them feels off. A prickle of unease crawls up my spine. My instincts kick in, telling me that there's more to this than meets the eye, so I follow them from a safe distance.

Moments later, I watch as they disappear down a dark corridor and then behind a heavy wooden door. Once I reach it, I instantly notice there's no sign like all the others. I place my ear up to the door and listen. When I do, I can hear muffled screams. Curiosity piqued, I gently push onto the door and peek inside. The room is bathed in a dim, otherworldly glow. Naked women, their faces hidden by intricate golden masks, circle two men who are bound and gagged. The air is thick with the scent of incense and something metallic, like blood.

Before I can take in more, a man in a mask steps forward, blocking my view. His eyes are cold and calculating, and I can sense the authority he holds in this room. Without a word, he closes the door in my face, the finality of it ringing in my ears.

My heartbeat quickens—a subtle alarm in the back of my mind. I take in the unsettling expanse of the dark, creepy hallway, shadows dancing along the walls. Something about this place feels off, as if unseen eyes are watching. I decide it is time to call it a night. The weight of my boots feels more pronounced now, each step echoing in the silence, signaling the end of a lucrative evening.

Back downstairs, I walk back through 'The Ruby Room,' weaving my way through the crowd and toward the exit. That's when I bump into him. I can't ignore the jolt of electricity that surges through my skin. I feel odd, nervous even. His face is covered by a white porcelain looking mask, covering everything but his eyes. Although I can't see his face, I'm sure that he is insanely handsome, tall, fit, all the things I would like if I were interested in romantic pursuits.

His eyes hold me in a trance, keeping me stuck in place. My heart begins to race once more, this time with a mixture of fear and excitement. Then he reaches out and gently takes my hand, leading me to the dance floor. Against all my rational judgment, I join him.

As our dance begins, the world falls away, leaving only the pulsing rhythm of desire and the enticing allure of the night. The music pulsates, creating an electric atmosphere that ignites every nerve in my body. Our connection feels magnetic, drawing me to him in a way I've never experienced before. It's intoxicating and confusing. Despite my curiosity about him—his name, his face—I suppress my urge to inquire. Instead, I embrace the freedom in anonymity, a liberation from the constraints of names and appearances.

Without a word, we lose ourselves in the rhythm, our bodies moving in perfect synchrony as if we're the only two people in the room. As the music shifts, I find my back pressed against his strong chest, his scent filling my senses. His touch sends shivers down my spine, igniting a fire within me that I can't deny.

I close my eyes and hold my breath as his fingers trail down my torso, brushing against my spot. Closing my eyes, I surrender to the sensation as his hands explore every inch of my body with tender urgency. When his fingers rub against my most private parts, surges of electricity course through my veins. I'm not used to relinquishing control—I'm usually the one who runs things. Yet, despite the inner conflict, I let myself be carried away by the pleasure. With a firm grip on his neck, the desire for more builds with each passing moment. Then, suddenly, a hint of reason creeps in, causing me to open my eyes. Before I can lose myself again, I tear away from his embrace, slipping through the crowd unnoticed.

Alone in my car, I steal a glance in the rearview mirror, still spinning from the encounter. This isn't like me. But something about tonight, about him, unraveled that. Even now, I can still feel his touch burned into my skin, like a brand. With a lingering desire to feel him on my lips, I disappear into the night, haunted by the memory of the stranger I danced with in the shadows.

CHAPTER

Five

COMING UP DEAD

Tempest

I't's a bright and early Monday morning, and the remnants of my now cold coffee sit abandoned on a coaster. I set my gaze on the screen before me, meticulously reviewing my notes on Karina Allegro's cold case. Having spent my weekend scouring through old tips, witness statements, and entries from my colleagues, I was hoping my fresh set of eyes would unearth any overlooked clues in this haunting case. But so far, I'm coming up painstakingly short.

As the time on my watch ticks by, I keep to the task. Deep down, I know it is only a matter of time before a new assignment lands on my desk. However, in the meantime, I type in the case number for Karina's case on my keyboard and diligently read through the case report once more.

"Allegro, Karina – (DOB 1/31/94) Female, Hispanic, 5'8, 160 pounds. On March 30, at 0612 hours, PPD was dispatched to the scene of a crime. The victim, later identified as Karina Allegro's body, was discovered under Interstate 76 overpass by construction workers. The body was decapitated, naked, and seemingly drained of blood. White rose petals were scattered over the body. The head has not been discovered. The coroner's office reports the cause of death: asphyxiation. Head was decapitated postmortem."

As my colleagues begin to trickle in, I stare at the crime scene photos spread across my desktop.

Maldonado enters, her exuberance evident as she carries a large pink box. "Good morning. Would you like a donut? They're fresh."

I indulge her kindness, reaching for a glazed donut. "Thank you," I respond, appreciating the gesture.

Maldonado beams in response. "You're welcome."

For a brief moment, I watch as she moves on to greet others, displaying a small beacon of warmth in the office. Her kindness will either make her time here a walk in the park or a living hell. Only time will tell.

Shrugging off the thought, I focus on my work. The images stare back at me, their haunting gaze a stark reminder of the horrors Karina endured in her final moments. Months have passed, yet the brutality of this crime speaks to a level of sadism that sends a shiver down my spine. In the pit of my stomach, I know the perpetrator will strike again; it's only a matter of time.

The photos that captured the scene are troublesome and odd. The place was expertly cleaned, just a torso covered in rose petals. I study them and quickly make a note of the precise staging the perpetrator accomplished. Given the fact that there was no blood at the scene and how her body was placed, this is not where she died, that I am most sure. But I struggle to understand the flower petals. Likely a mark or signature from the killer, I'm certain. A clear indication that whoever this sicko is takes pride in this kind of evil.

I take a seat and quickly jot down some notes in my notepad. The killer is deeply disturbed in some way, possibly with a personality disorder. And by looking at how clean the cut is, very skilled with a knife. Perhaps a surgeon or butcher of some sort.

Next, I look up Karina's information in the database. Karina faced minor charges, arrested two years ago for solicitation. She was young and very pretty. I wonder what made her life go left and take the wrong turn. I do a general search of her name to see if I can find any of her social media profiles or anything that will help me learn more about her.

"Dios mio, who would do such a thing?" Maldonado says upon her return to her desk.

It seems that her attempt to make nice with the team is working since the once-full donut box is now empty.

I sigh and nod. "Tell me about it."

Maldonado peeks over my shoulders to gain a better view of the photos. "People are truly fucking sick. Any luck with leads?"

"Not yet," I reply as I navigate to the public internet forum.

"Well, if you need help with anything, I'm more than happy to assist," she offers.

I smile. "I sure will, thanks."

A few hours later, I approach the doors of the Reading Terminal Market, a famed public market nestled in the heart of Center City, offering an array of sweets, dining, and farmer's market items. As I do, I see Fatima talking on her cell.

"No, Bryson, that's not going to work," she asserts.

I smile as I draw closer. I've come to admire her fearlessness. Something I bore witness to as we blossomed from young adolescents to adult women. It only takes her a moment to spot me crossing the intersection to join her.

"Bryson, I have to go. But I expect an update by the end of the day," she says before hanging up.

"Hey girl," I say.

We share a brief yet warm hug. Fatima has been one of my closest friends for as long as I can remember—honestly, she's been one of my only friends, aside from my sister. As a senior investigative journalist at *The Philadelphian Digest*, she prides herself on being a voice of reason and truth, with zero tolerance for bullshit. I'm so grateful to have her, especially when my life was falling apart. To be frank, I owe her my life.

It was her keen instincts that led her to check on me when I texted her about Lance dumping me. At that moment, she was the only person I could turn to, and her decision to come and check on me saved my life. She found me, nearly lifeless, sprawled across my bathroom floor and immediately called 911. What I love most about her is she never held that unfortunate incident over my head, not once. I feel safe with Fatima, much like I did with Jada.

Fatima beams, flashing a million-dollar smile complimented by a sharp designer trench coat and Italian leather boots.

Her hair is precisely cut and styled into a sleek bob, and her brown skin is flawless. "Temp! You look cute! How are you? How's the first week back?"

"So far, so good, but I do have some updates for you. You'll never guess who I ran into," I tease.

Her eyes instantly grow big. "No! Oh, my lord, are you serious?"

I nod. "Trust me, I wish that I wasn't."

We walk inside the busy market, heading straight to our favorite Thai stand to place our orders.

As we wait in the now-growing line, she turns her attention back on me, wasting no time to pry for more details. "So what happened?"

"Girl, the truth? I nearly shit myself," I whisper as I recount the last surprising encounter with my ex.

Fatima chuckles. "Oh my goodness! No, for real, what did you do? Slap him, I hope."

"I won't lie, I kind of wanted to. But no, I didn't do that. Hell, I've embarrassed myself enough. I kept my cool, but it was not easy," I confess.

She nods with complete understanding. "Did he say anything?"

I roll my eyes. "He asked me how I was."

"Seriously? Wouldn't he like to know," she says, reflecting my thoughts on the matter.

"Can I take your order?" the food attendant asks.

"Two salmon curry bowls, one with shrimp and both with extra curry sauce, please," Fatima says.

We pause to share a silent glance of excitement. It's been a little while since we indulged in our treasured rice bowls for lunch.

Continuing with my story, I explain, "I just said fine and went back to my desk, but I swear to you, I wanted to hide in the bathroom for the rest of the day."

"Shit, I'm sorry girl. I mean, we knew you were bound to run into him at some point. After all, he is a Chief DA now, right?"

"Yeah, I knew that it would happen soon enough," I say.

"But not this damn soon," Fatima adds.

We both share a laugh. Moments later, the attendant slides us our order. "That will be $22.86."

Fatima reaches into her purse, but before she can hand off her American Express card, the cashier is already swiping mine.

"Too slow." I give her a wink as she playfully nudges me with her elbow. We pick our food and walk to find an open table in the seating area.

As we settle into our seats, I continue, "I know. It was insane. But I refuse to let that man see me cry anymore."

She reaches out, touching my hand. "Well, I'm proud of you. The hard part is over, right?"

"Yes, I guess you're right. Truthfully, I don't think that I would've ever been ready, you know? I'm just glad that I managed to keep a pretty good poker face, I think."

The smell of the curry gives way, pulling us both in with the allure of deliciousness that we knew was in store. Ripping off the plastic wrapping of my utensils, I am eager to dive in.

After we both silently enjoy a few bites, I decide to shift the conversation, "So, what's up with you? Any news on the promotion?"

Fatima lets out a heavy, exasperated breath. A knowing sigh that many women, especially ones of darker hues, often face when navigating the complexities of the workplace.

"One more interview to go," she says. "I'm feeling pretty good about it, but you just never know, you know?"

I take another bite of my food and nod with understanding. Using my free hand, I cover my mouth to chew and swallow my lunch, then I say, "You know I get it, girl. But what else is new? Are you working on any cool articles? How'd that date go with that engineer?"

She rolls her eyes. "A complete waste of time. That man was a full-on narcissist, and I ended things as quickly as they started. He just couldn't handle the idea of dealing with a woman who wasn't overly impressed by his accolades and accomplishments."

Fatima's dating life is reminiscent of a reality show. Being an educated, beautiful, and successful woman has made her dating life challenging, but she refuses to give up—something I admire about her. As for me, I have no desire to trek down that road again. It's far too intimidating and depressing.

She continues, "But anyway, I am working on something very cool, actually. Did you know that over the last few years, some of the city's richest and most wealthy men have met a sudden and untimely death?"

That certainly captures my attention.

I quickly shake my head no. "That sounds creepy as hell."

"Tell me about it. Real estate moguls, philanthropists, doctors, you name it, dead, just like that," she says with an added snap of her fingers.

My eyebrow perches. "Like murdered, dead?"

She shakes her head. "That, my friend, is the great mystery. It's way too coincidental, don't you think? Is it merely bad luck, or is someone making these men disappear?" she teases.

"I'd hope if you come across any evidence of murder, you'd let me know?" I say.

Fatima chuckles. "You know if I did, I'd come running to you. Right now, I'd say it's more like bad luck, but if I come across anything substantial, you'll be the first to know. I've just got a few loose ends to tie up before it's published. I think I'm really onto something big here."

"Well, I can't wait to read it," I say.

Fatima smiles. "You're in for a treat, trust me."

I reply, "I wouldn't expect anything less."

She winks, and then her expression softens, "Have you heard from Jada lately? It's been so long since I've talked to her. Does she know about all of the great progress you've been making?"

My skin grows hot. The mention of my estranged sister's name sends my stomach into knots.

I swallow hard. "No, not since Ms. Gwen's funeral. She barely looked at me," I answer.

Losing Ms. Gwen to cervical cancer earlier this year was hard. I'm certain that it played a part in my mental break. Most of the kids she took in came to pay their respects and shower her with the love she deserved. Because of her, many of us were able to go out into the world and make something of ourselves—something I know gave her peace during her final days.

It was bittersweet, laying her to rest, loved and adored by so many. Mr. Lewis, her now-widowed husband, made sure to send her off like the queen she was. I had hoped to reconnect with Jada at the funeral, but she made it blatantly clear there was no chance for reconciliation. I continue eating my food, trying to keep my composure and burying those memories as best I can.

Just then, my phone rings, a relief from the tension I now feel. Placing my fork down, I reach into my pocket, pulling my cell out. "This is Detective Blaze," I answer.

"Blaze, this is Sterling. We've got the body of a man found. I want you to go check it out."

I smile. My first assignment since returning. "Yes, sir."

"Don't let me down," he says.

"I won't, sir."

I listen as he provides the address of the location, making note. "Copy that. I'll be right there."

I hang up my cell and then rise from my seat to grab my coat and badge, "Duty calls."

Fatima stands up, giving me a hug. "Okay, girl, you've got this! Let me know if you want to join me soon to work out. I've been going to this yoga class on Sundays, and it's amazing! I think you'd like it."

She looks into my eyes, pleading. I know that it's her way of getting me out of the house and away from work. Dr. Nelson insisted that I explore new and healthy ways to decompress and relax, so I say, "Sounds good, let's do it."

Fatima's face lights up. She's pleased. "It's a date!"

We hug once more before I retreat to my car, eager to dive into my first case since returning.

Twenty minutes later, I arrive at the crime scene, raindrops drumming a melancholic melody on the windshield.

Stepping out of my vehicle, I'm greeted by the familiar bustle of activity—a symphony of flashing lights, curious bystanders, and urgent voices. Retrieving my handheld voice recorder, I prepare to immerse myself in the grim task ahead.

Medics, patrol officers, and the crime scene unit swarm the area, each playing their part in the morbid dance of investigation. With a nod of acknowledgment, I exchange pleasantries with the team.

"Detective Blaze," Maldonado approaches, "I hope that you don't mind. Sergeant Sterling asked me to come and back you up."

I can sense her nervousness. "It's not a problem at all."

Although I suspect this is Sterling's way of keeping me on a leash, I resign to keeping those feelings to myself. During my time in the force, I was all too aware of how leadership often tried to pit women against one another. And that was at no fault of Maldonado's, she was just trying to do good police work. That I could sense, at least.

"Let's get started," I say, reaching into my back pocket. I pull out a pair of black latex gloves, carefully sliding them onto my hands, and she quickly mimics my movements. I turn to face the house of the apparent crime scene, taking in its modern architecture and surroundings.

Turning on my voice recorder, I quickly make note of everything I see. "Residence, Thirteen, Ravenwood Street. Four-story home in the Fairmount area. No signs of forced entry."

I can feel Maldonado watching me with intrigue, for she's getting the crash course in detective work that I'm sure she was yearning for. I ignore her gaze and continue on, briefly looking to the pavement for any potential clues. Then, I look at the neighboring homes on the small block. "Construction site across the street, house on the right appears to be a vacant property, and the building on the left is occupied. No cameras visible."

Once done, I turn my device off, reverting my attention back to Maldonado. "What's the situation?"

"Deceased is a Caucasian male. DOA. Name is Clay Winthrop, mid to late forties, owner of the property," she briefs me as we make our way past the yellow crime scene tape, up the stoop, and into the entryway of the residence.

Inside, the house is pristine, decorated with elegant furniture, textiles and artwork. Upon entering the foyer, I step into the living room. A grand piano is neatly positioned in the corner, and it's complimented by a fireplace. The home, adorned with lavish furnishings and tasteful decor, stands in stark contrast to the scene that has seemingly unfolded within its walls. By the main window sits a small bar displaying decanters filled with an array of aged scotch, cognac, and gin. My gaze sweeps over the room, searching for clues among the trappings of wealth.

Next, I walk back out into the main foyer, greeting more of my colleagues on the job when I do. A few paces ahead, I notice the main staircase, which faces the back of the house. As I draw closer, I see my victim lying lifeless at the foot of the steps. Walking over to the body, I take a moment to survey the scene.

My eyes flit over every detail, searching for any sign of disturbance or oddities. At first glance, it appears that his neck was broken as a result of the fall. I take in every detail, my mind racing to piece together the puzzle before me. My eyes closely scan the stairs that caused this man's untimely death. I see a glass on the second to last step. I reach over and pick it up, bringing the brim of the glass to the tip of my nose. When I do, I can instantly smell the remnants of cognac. I hand the glass to Bailey, a forensic analyst who's thorough and steadfast in her work. She takes the glass and places it into a plastic bag for testing later.

"Victim appears to have fallen down the stairs. Not very clear if it was intentional or accidental. No prevalent signs of foul play or defense wounds visible at this time."

Kneeling down, my eyes trail up the stairs and case the corners for surveillance cameras.

"Security footage?" I turn to Maldonado and ask.

"We're trying to locate that now," she explains.

Stepping around the body, I slowly make my way up the stairs, careful not to disturb anything. I carefully assess the walls and banister as I make my way up. Toward the middle of the stairwell, I see a cellphone, a possible clue. I pick it up and hand it to Maldonado, who is trailing close behind me along with Bailey.

Then, out of the corner of my eye, I see a Rolex watch under the console table at the top of the stairs. I kneel down, reaching out my hand to retrieve it. The clasp appears to have come undone, which is a possible sign of a struggle. I quickly make note of my findings and hand the watch to forensics for evidence.

I turn to Bailey. "Please be sure to dust all the doors and the banister for prints."

"We're on it, Detective," she says with a nod and proceeds to rejoin her team.

Maldonado follows me as I explore the second level of the home. But the bedrooms and bathrooms look undisturbed, as if he had just arrived home. "Any witnesses?" I inquire, my attention already turning to the task at hand.

"Just the housekeeper, Aya Lin," Maldonado responds. "She said that she comes to the property once a week to clean and didn't expect to see him here. Apparently, she walked in and found him dead at the bottom of the flight of stairs right before she started her shift."

As I step back into the foyer and walk into the kitchen of the property, Aya, the witness, sits nervously, wringing her hands, her eyes darting around the room.

"Ms. Lin, thank you for speaking with me," I begin, extending my hand.

I can sense her restlessness as she shakes my hand.

Keeping my tone gentle but firm, I continue, "I need to ask you about how you found Mr. Winthrop."

She nods, her eyes filled with a mix of apprehension and sadness. "Of course, Detective. I'll do my best to help."

"Can you walk me through what happened when you arrived this morning?" I ask, pen poised over my notebook.

"I came in a little after noon, maybe twelve fifteen, like I always do."

I nod. "Did anything seem out of place or strange upon arrival?"

Ms. Lin shakes her head. "No, the house was quiet, which is pretty normal. I was supposed to get the house cleaned and ready for new guests that would be arriving today. I started my cleaning, and then that's when I saw him at the bottom of the stairs," she says, her voice trembling slightly.

"You mentioned guests. Is this not Mr. Winthrop's permanent residence?" I ask.

She shakes her head. "No, this is a property he uses to temporarily rent to guests."

I quickly jot down some notes.

"Did you notice anything unusual before you found him? Anything out of place or signs of a struggle?" I ask.

She hesitates, brow furrowing. "Not really."

"Do you know why Mr. Winthrop was here instead of at his home?" I ask, intrigued.

Ms. Lin shifts uncomfortably. "Sometimes he has parties here, Detective. He rents this place out to guests, but sometimes he stays here to... get away, I think."

"Get away from what?" I probe.

"From Mrs. Winthrop, I suppose. Their marriage wasn't... happy. He often stayed here after their arguments," she explains.

"Thank you, Ms. Lin. You've been very helpful," I say as she turns to leave.

I step outside, piecing together the information, and turn to Maldonado, "Any word on the wife?"

"Not that I am aware of," she says.

Turning to her, I say, "Let's see if we can find and locate Mrs. Winthrop. We need to talk to her as soon as possible."

She nods. "On it."

As the coroner and medic team arrive to retrieve the body, I watch as they place it into the heavy-duty body bag and zip it closed.

"He's been deceased at least twelve hours," the coroner informs me, their words punctuating the heavy silence.

I press record. "Likely the victim died within the last day or so. The date is November 1."

Suddenly, the mention of the date sends a twitch of pain in my heart, as it is the eve of Jada's birthday. With a sigh, I bury those troublesome feelings and resume my examination of the surroundings, methodically combing through every inch of the house for any shred of evidence. But despite my efforts, the trail remains frustratingly cold.

The glare of the news vans pulling up signals the arrival of unwanted attention. I ready myself for the challenges that lie ahead. In a case like this, every detail matters, every clue a potential breakthrough. And as the investigation unfolds, I know that only time will reveal the secrets hidden within these walls.

CHAPTER

Six

THE PERFECT GENTLEMAN

Stormy

Today, I quietly turn thirty-three, but I don't make a big deal of it. Truth is, I was never much into celebrating my birthday. I figured a nice day at the spa would be enough. But as I navigate the late morning traffic en route to my appointment, I'm compelled to take a slight detour.

As I drive through the treacherous streets, I catch a glimpse of a familiar figure—my mother. It's a sobering reminder of the underlying forces at play, the same ones that kept her from fulfilling her maternal duties for much of my life.

I did it. I graduated from high school. As the crowd erupts in applause, I scan the sea of faces, searching for the one I longed to see, my mother's. I wanted her to see me in this moment, to see that I made it and was well on my way toward making something of myself.

My cap sits on top of my head, the tassel lightly brushing against my cheek as I continue looking out into the crowd. I spot Ms. Gwen and Mr. Lewis waving at me. I smile and wave back. Although I am so grateful to them both, I want nothing more than to see my own mother walking through those doors, to know that she'd finally show up for me—for us. But as the minutes drag on and the ceremony draws to a close, reality settles in like a weight in my chest. She isn't coming.

Just then, Tempest reaches out her hand, lacing her fingers with mine. I look at my best friend, my sister, initially bound by trauma and tragedy, and force a smile. She gives my hand a gentle squeeze and a wink. I quickly brush away my tears and wink back.

Despite her many mistakes and countless disappointments, I can't help but still long for my mother's love and embrace. I know the demons she battles have a suffocating grip on her, one much stronger than the love she has for me.

I watch as she sits on an empty stoop, her hair and clothes dirty and disheveled, seemingly disconnected from reality. With a heavy heart, I park my car and approach her.

"Hey, Ma," I say.

It takes her a few moments to register my voice. When she finally does, she slowly turns her gaze to me. "Jada, is that my Jada?"

"Yes, it's me," I say softly.

A smile of happiness and relief spreads across her face, but it quickly fades into shame as she hangs her head, staring down at the pavement. "I don't want you seeing me like this."

"I know. I just wanted to check on you," I admit, my voice trembling slightly.

"I'm all right, baby. I'm all right. The devil ain't take me yet," she says, her tone trying to be reassuring but faltering under the weight of her reality.

My lip quivers as I take in the current state of my mother, her appearance more ravaged than the last time I saw her. It seems that each time she falls off the rails, her descent into darkness is deeper and worse than before. It's hard to see her like this, and I'm eager to leave. I take a deep breath and offer her some money—a small gesture in the face of her mounting struggle.

A LITTLE WHILE LATER, I STEP INTO THE OPULENT LOBBY OF THE luxurious Black Retreat spa, and a wave of tranquility washes over me. The air is infused with the soothing scent of lavender, and soft instrumental music plays in the background, creating a serene atmosphere. As I approach the reception desk, I see Cherelle, or Paige, as she now likes to call herself, waiting. Her perfectly manicured nails tap impatiently on the marble countertop.

"Finally, I was beginning to think you got lost on the way here," Paige says with a playful smirk and eye roll.

I chuckle softly, the tension of the outside world melting away as I join her. "Sorry, traffic was a nightmare," I lie.

It's surprising how far Paige and I have come since our early days filled with teenage rivalries. After that momentous summer day, I never had to deal with her bullying again. Over time, our dispute evolved into mutual respect, which lasted through the end of high school.

Then, one fateful day, I was window shopping at a designer store, dreaming of a future where I could finally afford such luxury. Having just dropped out of college after only attending one semester, I figured life would be a better and cheaper teacher than those predatory schools. I did hair to get by, but I quickly found myself broke and eager to find a way to a path filled with purpose. Then, there she was, Cherelle, walking through the store with a wealthy-looking man on one arm and a handful of the latest designer fashions in the other.

We quickly connected and exchanged numbers. Within a few days, I was completely sucked into her world, filled with money, expensive dinners, luxurious trips, and very well-to-do men. I was enamored by the promise of becoming the financially secure woman I'd dreamed of for so long. So, I followed suit, fully immersing myself in this alluring lifestyle. Naively hoping that my sacrifice would lead me to meet a man who could help me make my dreams a reality.

I can still remember my first client, Hugo, a powerful marketing executive visiting from Los Angeles. He quickly drew me in, making promises to help me start anew and become the superstar I always knew I was destined to be. After a night of wining, dining, and doing what I deemed necessary, I woke up in his extravagant hotel room, naked and alone. An envelope containing one thousand dollars sat on the nightstand. I cried like a baby, ashamed and embarrassed, unable to tell anyone, not even Tempest. I knew that she would never understand this type of lifestyle and wouldn't hesitate to express her concerns and disapproval.

So, I turned to Paige, a person that I still don't completely trust. But she understood this life, and it's the secret that has bound us to this day. She helped me dry my tears and taught me the game of providing fantasy and the art of seduction. Over time, I slowly built my confidence, shedding my name and my past along with it. Finally emerging as Stormy, my fearless and tantalizing alter ego. It didn't take long to build a clientele filled with generous lovers and sugar daddies. Things worked out quite differently than I had planned, for I never became the star I had always wanted to be, but I'm not complaining. After spending a few years depending on men to shape my fate, I decided to take my destiny into my own hands and flip the script. Using their arrogance, affluence, and ego against them, I have no regrets. Embracing my role as Stormy, I have carved out a life of independence and control, turning the tables on those who once held power over me.

Paige took a different path, shedding the extra body weight, lightening her skin, and entrusting the best surgeons to completely alter her look. She quickly attracted and wedded a very wealthy and much older man. Then, after four years of marriage and a life of domestication, her husband, Dominic Hansen, suddenly dropped dead due to heart complications just a year before. Now, she is a widow, a widow, living off her husband's extremely lavish estate.

Lately, her days have been filled with enjoying the fruits of her newfound wealth and making her best attempts to rub elbows with the city's most elite. In contrast, my days consist of calculated moves and strategic encounters, each step meticulously planned to preserve my freedom and attain wealth on my own terms.

Upon checking in, we make our way through the spa, passing by bubbling hot tubs and steam rooms filled with swirling clouds of mist. We settle in a secluded corner of the changing room, where plush robes and slippers await us. As I slip out of my clothes into the soft fabric, I can feel the stresses of the day fall away with each passing moment. We spend the next few hours catching up as we indulge in luxurious massages and rejuvenating facials.

In the sauna, I inquire about Paige's latest happenings. It's been some time since we've caught up. "How was Turks?"

She smiles but keeps her eyes closed, a clear indication that she enjoyed herself. "Turks was a dream. You should go! There are a lot of rich, lonely men. You'd eat them right up!"

I giggle. "Although that sounds tempting, I think I may give that all up. I'm ready to move on."

That confession snatches her full attention, causing her to sit up and look at me. "What do you mean, give it up? Give it up and do what?"

"I was considering acting, maybe taking some classes." I shrug.

Paige lets out a hearty, dismissive laugh. "Bitch, you've been an actress. What do you think all this is? It's an act."

"Yeah, I know. I'm just tired of all the games. It gets old after a while," I confess.

"Well, I told you to get smart and marry one of them and get set up for good," Paige says.

I sigh. "I don't know how I feel about that."

Paige counters, "Don't tell me you're waiting for love."

I shrug. "I don't know. What if I am? Would that be so horrible? It's not like I can carry on like this forever. I need an exit plan."

She laughs again, and I grow irritated. "How many times do I have to tell you that women like us don't love? We survive. Have you forgotten?"

I shake my head. "No, I know that. I just am starting to understand that there's more to life than simply surviving and money."

"I know what it is. That psycho chick going ham and killing your friends got you scared," she charges.

I take a sip of my champagne. Through all of her surgeries, Paige still hasn't quite shed her mean-girl spirit.

"You still doing what you do?" Paige pries. She's the only other person who knows about my extracurricular activities.

I sip my champagne again.

"See, that's what's got you all scary and shit. Get you a husband, girl, and leave that shit behind. Drugging and stealing from folks is what's going to get you caught up, not marrying a man that wants to trick on you."

"What else is new with you?" I ask, eager to change the subject.

"Oh, nothing besides the fact that Dom's brother is in town minding my damn business," she says, her irritation blatantly clear.

"What's that about?" I ask.

Her face flattens. "Who knows, probably trying to dictate how I'm spending his brother's money."

We both share a laugh and take a sip of our champagne.

"Little does he know; those days are over. I'll never allow a man, or anyone for that matter, to control my life ever again," Paige announces.

Often, women are enticed by the glitz and glamour of our lifestyle, but they fail to grasp the sacrifices and, at times, the dangers that have been endured to attain a certain level of affluence. But I knew all too well.

Paige had always been ambitious, but something had shifted in her over these last few months. Tired of playing by the rules, tired of relying on men, she was ready to take more control of her destiny, and she'd realized that her power didn't lie in trying to be some rich man's play thing. Now, she set her sights on building connections with powerful women, understanding that they could open doors that had been shut in her face for far too long.

"Cheers to that!" I say, holding my glass up.

She smiles before tapping her glass with mine. By the time our spa day comes to an end, I feel completely renewed and rejuvenated, ready to enjoy the rest of my day.

Later that evening, Ashton's is filled with its usual crowd of male patrons being served by young and bright-eyed waitresses. At the bar, I pick up my dirty martini, take a sip, and focus on the television screens before me. There are four large displays evenly spaced throughout the cigar lounge. The basketball game being played by the hometown 76ers team is playing on all screens except one. I'm not much into sports, so I settle on the only television showing the news.

"Hey babe, are you doing all right?" Seven, my friendly bartender asks.

I smile and nod. "Yes, I'm good."

Seven continues, "What brings you in here on a Tuesday night?"

"It's my birthday," I confess with a hint of reluctance.

Her eyes grow big with excitement. "What! Happy birthday, girl. This calls for a round of shots on me. Is tequila all right?"

Before I can stop her, Seven busies herself, pouring two shots and sliding one toward me, "Here."

We tap our glasses together. "Cheers."

After we take our shots, Seven excuses herself to attend to her other patrons. I pick up my Panatela cigar and bring it to my lips, drawing in a puff. The sensation of the rich yet complex burst of flavor coating my mouth. Careful not to inhale the smoke, I savor the taste for a moment, then slowly blow it out.

Through the wireless speakers, "Journey to Atlantis" by The Isley Brothers plays softly in the background. I close my eyes, lean my head back, and briefly lose myself in the music. Softly snapping my fingers and humming the chorus. When I open my eyes, I can see the men in the bar watching me, but I don't care. It's not often they see a woman alone at a cigar lounge enjoying a drink and cigar all by herself.

Just then, Seven approaches with another dirty martini, placing it atop a paper coaster and gliding it in front of me.

My eyebrow arches. "I didn't order this."

Seven winks. "I know, someone asked me to pour it for you. They said you look like you could use it, and honestly, I agree."

I smile. "Who?"

She nods her head to her left and in the direction of a handsome gentleman seated alone in the corner. He holds his glass up, and I do the same, toasting our drinks. Although he's cute, I'm not too interested in engaging with the opposite sex today. I do that enough for a living and am entitled to a night off, especially on my birthday.

"Long day?" Seven asks, crossing her arms under herself and leaning on top of the bar, showcasing an intricate botanical tattoo that wraps around her wrist.

I sip my new cocktail. "More like long life. But that's a whole other conversation. How have you been?" I ask, eager to change the subject.

She sighs. "Good, school is kicking my ass and then some."

"Stick to it. It will all be worth it in the end, trust me. Why don't you pour yourself a drink and put it on his tab," I instruct her.

She laughs and does just that. "Here's hoping."

We tap our glasses together once more. "Cheers."

Then, over her shoulder, I see the breaking story on the news. I take another sip of my drink and watch, horrified, as the headline reads, **"Philadelphia Police: Body of man found identified as Philly Real Estate Mogul."**

I nearly spit out my drink when Clay's photo flashes onto the screen. My head begins to spin with what feels like a million questions. My eyes look at the television again, trying to confirm that this isn't a dream. When I do, my stomach drops as I see my sister, Tempest, in the background. She looks poised, focused, and beautiful, yet seeing her face is like a punch to the gut.

It still saddens me how we've ultimately become strangers, given how close we once were. I wish her nothing but the best, but I fear that things are beyond repair. Despite what has transpired between us, I'm damn proud of her. If anyone deserves to be happy, it's her. I just hope that's actually the case.

I quickly take another sip of my drink, swallowing my thoughts and feelings along with it. I don't want to be bogged down by the past. Instead, I divert my attention to the basketball game. I spend the next few minutes distracting myself, watching the patrons of the lounge and averting their romantic passes.

An hour later, I step out of the lounge and into the night, opting to forgo a ride and take the quick walk home. The crisp nighttime air after the short rain storm calms my tangled thoughts. I tug the straps of my coat tighter around my waist and weave through the sea of people now flooding the streets.

As I walk, I keep to myself, careful not to get caught in the waves of the crowd. The city's pulse is electric, a blend of honking cars, distant boos, and the occasional shouts of disgruntled fans. Unfortunately, the hometown team lost the high-stakes basketball game, and Philadelphia fans are infamous for their passion and anger. The disappointment in the air is palpable, a mix of frustration and defiance.

The neon lights of the bars and restaurants blur together, casting a colorful glow onto the wet pavement. I manage to dodge a couple of overly enthusiastic fans, their jerseys drenched in rain, sweat, and beer, their faces flushed with a mix of alcohol and defeat. But as the sidewalks grow more congested, I decide to detour onto Sansom, a small street with much less action.

Each step seems to echo my internal struggle, the rhythmic tapping of my heels on the sidewalk a reminder of the night's revelations. I take a deep breath, letting the cold air fill my lungs, hoping it will help clear my mind. But as I walk, a strange feeling washes over me—an eerie chill creeping up my spine. I can't shake the sensation that someone is following me.

I glance over my shoulder, keeping my pace steady, trying not to let on that I'm aware. In the shadows, I catch sight of a figure wearing a black cap pulled low, their face covered by the darkness. I can't make out any details, but the unease deepens, gnawing at the edges of my nerves.

Instinct kicks in as I reach into my clutch, wrapping my fingers around my handgun. I start walking faster, my pulse quickening with each step. I turn a corner, eager to make my escape, but before I can make a run for it, I slam into a chest— solid, unyielding, like a brick wall. The collision jolts me, and I stumble back, my heel snapping, sending me crashing to the pavement.

Pain shoots through my knee, and a burning sensation spreads across my palm, likely scraped during the fall. Panic floods over me as I quickly glance over my shoulder to see if the mysterious figure is close. But to my relief, he's gone, as if he evaporated into the night air like a ghost. I let out a soft sigh as the seeming brick wall I crashed into bends down and helps me to my feet.

"Thank you," I manage to say, my voice shaky.

My heart nearly skips a beat when our eyes meet.

"I'm so sorry. I didn't see you," his voice says.

"It's okay, I was a bit distracted," I say with another glance over my shoulder.

He smiles. "That was a pretty nasty fall you took."

I nod, trying to shake off the embarrassment. "Yeah, I don't know what hurts more, my knee or my pride."

He chuckles, revealing perfectly white teeth. "It happens to the best of us. Here, let me help you."

The stranger guides me over to a vacant stoop, helping me take a seat on the cool, damp gravel. That's when I notice the blood trickling down my leg. Without hesitation, he reaches into his coat pocket, pulls out a handkerchief, and uses it to wipe up the blood. Now that I'm seated, I fully take him in, noticing the small digital camera hanging around his neck. He's extremely handsome, his skin reminiscent of a glazed pecan, his wavy hair well-groomed, and his beard perfectly tapered.

"Are you a photographer? Thank goodness you didn't capture that." I say, mortified.

The corner of his lip curls. "I liken myself to be, but truthfully, it's just a meaningless hobby. And don't worry, your fall will be a faded memory soon enough."

I let out a soft, relieved laugh.

"Looks like a pretty harmless cut," he says, examining my knee.

"Yeah, it should heal okay," I reply, grateful for his kindness.

"I'm Zayn," he says, extending a hand.

I reach out, placing my hand into his. "Stormy."

"How do you feel?"

"I'm all right for the most part," I say, a twinge of embarrassment still tickling my skin.

He watches me carefully. "Are you sure you'll be able to get to wherever you're going on that thing?"

We both look down at my broken heel, and I let out a nervous laugh. "I believe so."

"Do you mind if I see you off to wherever you were going? I can't, in good conscience, let you walk alone, given your condition and the recent news headlines," he asks, seemingly the perfect gentleman.

"I can manage," I say.

After all, I don't know this man, he could be a damn serial killer or something.

"Let me get you a ride. It's the least I can do," Zayn offers.

I contemplate his proposition for a moment. He does have a point. "That would be nice. Thank you."

I watch as he waves down a taxi, a dying artifact in the city as of late. He grabs my hand, helping me inside the car.

"Can I have your number?" he asks before closing the door.

His forwardness takes me by surprise. "Sure," I say. All things considered, bumping into him might've just saved my life. I figure a few friendly conversations wouldn't hurt. Maybe it would be worth my while.

I take his phone, typing my name and phone number in before handing it back to him.

"Thanks again," I say before my taxi pulls off, and I give him the details of my destination. Looking over my shoulder, I smile at the perfect stranger in the distance.

CHAPTER
Seven

THE MOGUL AND HIS WIFE

Tempest

Wednesday morning, the sun filters through the large windows of the gym, casting a golden glow on the familiar space. The rhythmic thud of gloves hitting heavy bags fills the air, blending with the low hum of conversation and the occasional grunt of effort. I take a deep breath, the scent of sweat and leather filling my lungs, grounding me in the moment. It's been over a year since I last set foot in this place, but the sense of familiarity feels surprisingly nice.

I wrap my hands with the familiar strips of cloth; the action is as instinctual as breathing. The tension that's been coiled tight within me begins to unwind, the simple act of preparing for class bringing a sense of normalcy I've greatly missed. I glance around the room, spotting a few faces I recognize, but most are new—a reminder of how much time has passed.

As the class begins, I find myself slipping into the rhythm, the controlled aggression of each punch and jab helping to release the pent-up energy that's been swirling inside me. It feels good—better than I expected—to do something familiar, to channel my frustration and anxiety into something physical. Each punch lands with satisfying precision, the sound echoing off the walls, reminding me of the strength I still possess.

"Nice form, Tempest. Glad to see you back," a deep voice calls out, pulling me from my focus. I turn to see the gym's owner, Andre, standing nearby with a wide grin on his face.

"Thanks, Andre," I reply, trying to keep my breathing steady. "It's good to be back."

After class, I use my hand towel to wipe the sweat from my forehead before stuffing it into my gym bag. As I prepare to leave, Andre approaches, his chiseled physique visible through his T-shirt.

"It's been too long," he says, stepping closer.

"Life got in the way," I say, brushing off the past year with a vague explanation. "But it feels good to do something familiar again."

"Well, I'm glad you're here," he says, his voice warm. "You've still got it. And you changed your hair, I like it." His eyes, a rich shade of brown with hints of honey, seem to sparkle with something more than just friendliness.

As I pull on my coat, I can't help but smile, feeling a warmth spread through me that has nothing to do with the workout. Is he flirting with me?

"I'm sure you're just saying that to be nice, but thank you," I say, trying to downplay the flutter in my chest.

Andre laughs, revealing a boyish grin. I'm not sure if it's the time that's passed or if I was too consumed by Lance before, but he's extremely attractive—something I'm sure every woman who crosses his path is keenly aware of.

"Well, I hope you'll be back soon," he says, his tone genuinely hopeful.

"I sure will," I reply, my voice a little softer this time.

He holds my gaze for a moment longer than necessary before giving me a nod. "See you around, Temp," he says before turning to help another member with their technique.

LATER THAT MORNING, I TAKE A SIP OF MY BROWN SUGAR AND vanilla latte and proceed to pull into the parking lot of the police district, eager to dive into my new case. But when I do, I'm shocked to see a police cruiser blocking my designated parking spot. I pull up beside him and honk my horn to capture his attention.

When I do, I greet him with a smile. "Good morning. Do you mind moving up? You're blocking my space."

His demeanor is indifferent, annoyed even. "There's plenty of other open spots in here. Find somewhere else to park."

The dismissiveness in his tone is undeniable, but I refuse to back down. I'd earned that parking spot, given my successes in the homicide division. I say, "Excuse me?"

Without hesitation, I put my car into park and get out to approach him and get his name, but when I do, the bastard pulls off and out of the garage.

"Jerk," I mutter to myself before getting back into my vehicle and dutifully pulling into my parking space.

Inside, I take a seat at my desk, intentionally letting the sour encounter fall by the wayside. Logging into my computer, I pull up my emails and see an update regarding the security cameras we retrieved from the property. But when I read the summary provided by the crime scene analysis team, slight frustration bubbles within me. Since the property is used as a rental space, numerous fingerprints were found, making it difficult to pinpoint any anomalies. It's also a dead end with the surveillance tapes. Unfortunately, the security cameras were never properly installed. Yielding no clues to the events leading up to Clay's demise.

Hoping to uncover some hidden connection or overlooked detail, I listen to my voice recordings, making notes of items to follow up on. As I delve into various online records, I construct a profile of the deceased, piecing together his past successes and present circumstances.

Before long, Clay's life story unfolds before me like a carefully crafted novel. Forty-eight years old, married, no children, a Harvard graduate who moved to the city over a decade ago and warped into a real estate titan with a seemingly charmed existence. To all appearances, everything about Clay's life, and ultimately, death, fit into a makeshift cookie-cutter puzzle. Except for the watch—why was that Rolex on the floor and not on his wrist? Given its quality and price, it's not something one would carelessly toss aside.

I hoped that news of Clay's death would generate some leads, but so far, there's been nothing. Even when I initially spoke to his wife, Quinn Winthrop, she didn't have much insight to offer. She was visibly shaken and distraught when

Maldonado and I delivered the news, so I didn't want to pry too hard or too soon with my follow-up questions.

Instead, I decided to try to understand as much as I could about the mogul and his wife. In my efforts, I quickly learned that Quinn is a figure shrouded in mystery despite her public presence—a woman of philanthropy and influence. Accordinging to my research, the two were a powerhouse couple with a seemingly happy marriage on the surface.

But, if that was the case, why was he found at a rental property instead of the home they shared? And why did Ms. Lin give any indication that their marriage was estranged?

Determined to uncover the truth, I dial up Mrs. Winthrop's number, my heart pounding with anticipation. After a few rings, an unfamiliar voice picks up.

"Hello? This is Detective Tempest Blaze with the Philadelphia Police's homicide division. Can I please speak to Quinn Winthrop?" I ask, my words a delicate dance of diplomacy and urgency.

"Mrs. Winthrop isn't available at the moment," she coolly says.

Before I can respond, the phone line goes dead. I pull the phone away from my ear, staring at it for a moment before hanging up. Just as I do, Maldonado strides into the room. Her energy is unmistakable, even in our bleak surroundings. Normally, I appreciate her bright aura and lightness, but today, it's just grating on my nerves.

"Good morning, Blaze," Maldonado beams, her optimism almost contagious… almost.

"Hey, Maldonado, can you see what financial records you can find on Clay Winthrop?" I ask, turning my attention back to the case. I'm determined to put together the puzzle of Clay's death, no matter how many pieces are missing.

By the end of the night, I manage to get my hands on some of his financial records, and what I find sends a chill down my spine. Hidden among the legitimate transactions from his real estate empire are red flags—large sums of money being funneled through shell companies, offshore accounts tied to shady developments, and property deals that don't add up. The deeper I look, the clearer it becomes—Clay wasn't just flipping properties; he was flipping the script on what it means to stay clean in the real estate game.

Fraud, money laundering, and—if my sources are correct—a possible connection to the mob. This wasn't just some white-collar crime; this was the kind of dirty business that could easily get a man killed. The more I piece together, the more it seems like Clay was neck-deep in a scheme that was bound to catch up with him sooner or later.

I can't shake the feeling that there's something bigger at play here, something that goes beyond a domestic dispute or a random act of violence. It looks like Clay was tangled up in a world of crime and corruption that led to his downfall, his empire built on shaky ground. My gut tells me this isn't just a simple murder; it's someone trying to cover their tracks.

Maybe Clay got too greedy, maybe he crossed the wrong people in one of his high-stakes deals, and they decided to take him out before he could do more damage. But still, there's a nagging doubt. The pieces don't fit together as neatly as I'd like. I've been around long enough to know that in cases like this, the truth is often buried under layers of deception.

THE EVENING IS DRAPED IN A SOMBER FOG AS I APPROACH THE Winthrop mansion, its imposing structure tucked away in the leafy confines of Chestnut Hill. The grandness of its facade casts a shadow onto the street. With a steady hand, I press the doorbell, its chime echoing through the silent corridors within.

Moments later, Mrs. Winthrop greets me with a composed expression, though a glimmer of unease flickers in her eyes. Her demeanor is poised and calm, far from the grieving widow I had expected. "Detective," she acknowledges, inviting me into the opulent foyer.

"Mrs. Winthrop, thank you for agreeing to meet with me on such short notice," I say, stepping inside.

Navigating the plush interior, we settle into her luxurious living room. She gestures for me to have a seat.

Without hesitation, I delve into the heart of the matter. "Mrs. Winthrop, please accept my condolences once again," I begin, my voice steady yet probing. "I'm here because I have some follow-up questions regarding your husband's recent passing."

She crosses her legs and lights a thin cigarette. "I don't know how much help I can be. My husband was diligent about keeping his secrets."

"Are you suggesting he had something to hide?"

"If he did, I'm certain I wouldn't know about it," she replies.

I press further. "Did Mr. Winthrop have any enemies or recent disagreements that he mentioned?"

She shakes her head. "No, nothing out of the ordinary—just work-related stuff, if anything."

"Mrs. Winthrop, there's no easy way to ask this, but how well did you really know your husband?"

Her eyes narrow slightly. "What makes you ask that?"

"I have reason to believe he was involved in some shady business dealings."

She remains silent, the only response being a slow drag from her cigarette.

"When was the last time you saw your husband alive?" I inquire, sensing a guardedness in her demeanor.

"Saturday morning, before I left for New York."

"What was in New York?" I ask.

"A charity for cancer research. I am on the board of directors," she explains.

"When you saw Mr. Winthrop, did you notice anything out of the ordinary? Did he seem sick or upset at all?" I study her carefully, noting the subtle shifts in her body language.

Quinn's gaze wavers for a brief moment before regaining its composure. "No, nothing out of the ordinary," she asserts, her tone tinged with restraint.

"Mrs. Winthrop, do you have any reason to suspect that someone would want your husband dead?" I ask.

I can tell that I've struck a chord. "Excuse me, what? You think my husband was murdered?"

"I'm just doing my due diligence, ma'am. Until I receive the official autopsy report, I will not rule out the possibility."

"Well, that's utterly ridiculous," she snorts.

I remain calm and rise from my chair, "I think that I have everything I need for now. But please, if you think of anything else, give me a call."

I reach into my blazer pocket and pull out a business card with my information. She nods and places it down on the coffee table without so much as a glance.

When we approach the door, I step outside and turn back to her. "I will be sure to keep you updated on any breaks in the case. Thank you for your time."

Mrs. Winthrop says, "Thank you," before gently closing the door in my face.

As I step back out into the night and walk to my car, I can't shake the feeling that there's more to Quinn's story than meets the eye, especially since she stood to inherit fifty million dollars from his death.

THE NEXT DAY, THE MORNING SUN CASTS A WARM HUE OVER THE city as I make my way to the coroner's office, the weight of unresolved questions heavy on my mind. Stepping into its sterile confines, I'm greeted by the brisk efficiency of the staff going about their duties.

It doesn't take me long to spot James, the medical examiner assigned to the case, heading toward his desk with a hardened look of exhaustion on his face. When he sees me, his expression softens a bit. "Blaze! It's been quite some time. Welcome back."

"Thank you, James. How have you been?" I ask.

"Miserable," he says with a laugh as he slips on his lab jacket. "My new girlfriend is a six on a good day, and I'm still stuck in this shit hole."

James has always had a unique outlook on life. Being surrounded by so much death has made his dark humor almost automatic.

He continues, "To what do I owe this pleasure? I know you didn't miss me that much to be paying me personal visits."

"Any updates on the autopsy of Clay Winthrop?" I inquire, my eyes fixed on the files piled on top of his desk.

He takes a seat and meets my gaze with a solemn nod. "Our findings indicate that Mr. Winthrop's death was attributed to sudden cardiac arrest," he states matter-of-factly.

My brow furrows in disbelief, a sense of frustration bubbling within me. "A heart attack?"

He nods. "Looks like that caused the fall."

"What about the discarded watch? How would he have had enough time to remove it if he was having a heart attack?" I interject, my voice filled with skepticism.

"I guess that he could have removed it before it happened," he replies indifferently.

I nod. "Is there any way to find out if he had a history of a heart condition?"

James's expression softens, understanding the gravity of the situation. "We'll need to conduct further tests to confirm our findings," he concedes, a note of uncertainty tainting his words.

"What about the toxicology report?"

He explains, "The team is pretty backed up, but I suspect we'll have something in the next couple of days."

My brows furrow, frustration mounting within me. "All right, thank you. Please let me know as soon as you get word."

"You bet ya," James says.

As I depart from the coroner's office, the inconsistencies of the situation gnaw at me. Heart attack? It doesn't add up—not with the evidence I've gathered thus far. Determined to uncover the truth, I resign myself to waiting for the toxicology report, hoping that answers lie within the meticulous analysis of Clay's final moments.

CHAPTER
Eight

A HINT OF VANILLA

Stormy

My grip tightens on the steering wheel as I navigate through Kensington, a neglected corner of the city where people are abandoned to wither away. I've always harbored a deep disdain for this part of town. The city's attempt to designate it a drug-free zone years ago feels like a distant memory, overshadowed by the current situation. It's a stark reminder of the cyclical nature of urban decay, a haunting echo of the crack epidemic that ravaged communities in the past. Now, the streets are overrun with what I can only describe as zombies—the methamphetamine addicts left to waste away in plain sight.

My focus remains on the road ahead, and my senses are heightened for any signs of danger that could be lurking. In this neighborhood, chaos can erupt at a moment's notice, and I refuse to let my guard down. The recent news of Clay's death has left me feeling unsettled and confused. When I left Clay, he was very much alive. What are the chances he suddenly turns up dead? Had I taken things too far and given him too many drugs? Had my concoction taken a while to leave his system?

No theory seemed to make any sense. I've never had someone turn up dead before, not once. Since the news broke, I've been glued to updates, hungry for any scrap of information. Right now, it's clear I need to keep a low profile until this whole mess blows over. I can't bring myself to believe that I could be capable of such a thing. I'm a lot of things, but I'm not a killer. I refuse to let my mind even entertain that dark, sick possibility. Instead, I'm focused on the pressing task at hand: getting rid of the items I snagged on Halloween night and getting my hands on as much money as I can. As it appears, I'll be leaving Philly much sooner than I anticipated.

I pull up to Zee's house and reach for my bag, my findings securely hidden within its pockets. In this part of town, you don't want to draw too much attention to yourself, or you'll instantly become a target. I chose sneakers and a sweatsuit instead of my usual stilettos, trench coat, and one of my many designer bags. I take a moment to adjust my baseball cap and put on large sunglasses with the hopes of being discreet.

Zelda Marie Jones has been my trusted business associate for all my less-than-legal dealings over the last few years. A half-Black, half-Puerto Rican high school dropout turned prostitute, then drug dealer, and now the queen of the underground—at least in Philly. When it comes to selling on the black market or getting rid of things that could bring heat, Zee is the ultimate professional.

Though it's unclear how she built such a lucrative business, word has it she controls a network spanning from DC to New York. A hidden conglomerate of making things disappear, cleaning money, and pretty much any other illegal dealing you can think of. Zee is the epitome of a boss and a perfect ally. Once close friends with my mother, she'd taken a strong liking to me as a young girl, granting me wisdom and protection. She understands my world, and I have tremendous respect for her. People know not to mess with her or her people, and I am one of her girls. I trust Zee as much as you can trust any criminal, but I respect her work ethic. She runs a tight operation, is good at keeping secrets, and is fair.

I set my sights on the old house tucked in the middle of Amber Street, one of the blocks Zee owns through agreements with neighbors, promising protection and no riffraff. As expected, a group of men stands guard on the porch.

"Damn, sis, you bad as shit. You got Indian in you?" one of them asks.

Ignoring his question, I say, "I'm here for Zee. Tell her it's Jada."

One of the guys slips into the house to deliver my message. I wait patiently, ignoring the gawks and lustful glances. Moments later, he returns, granting me access inside the house and leading me downstairs into the finished basement.

Zee sits at a large table, a cigarette in her mouth and a cocktail glass in her hand. Her hair is styled impeccably in a Dominican blow-out, and she dons a designer top and matching slacks. When she sees me, she instantly smiles.

"Well, isn't it one of my favorite customers? What can I do for you, suga?" she says, rising to give me a warm hug.

I walk over to the table and join her. I reach into my purse, pulling out the items I swiped: a Rolex watch, credit cards, and other jewelry, placing them in front of her.

Zee puts on her glasses and examines the items carefully. When she picks up the watch, she studies its makeup. "I'll give you ten for it."

I know she's lowballing me. This watch retails for at least twenty thousand dollars, and she could sell it for at least seventeen. I'm not trying to be greedy, but I have to stand my ground.

"Sixteen," I counter.

The corner of her mouth turns up, amused. She examines it more closely for a few more moments. "Fourteen," she says.

I think it over for a second before nodding. "Deal."

By the end of the ordeal, I had secured twenty thousand dollars. Zee takes a sip of her cocktail and turns to her associate. "Juan, get me twenty stacks."

"How much is a new ID and passport?" I ask before he walks away.

Zee raises an eyebrow. "Finally getting out of town?"

I nod. "I'm strongly considering it."

"I don't blame you. Nothing here but trouble. How soon do you need it?" she asks.

"As soon as possible," I admit.

"Two thousand," she replies.

I nod. "Let's do it. Thanks, Zee."

She winks and turns back to Juan. "Make that eighteen stacks for me, honey."

The man disappears into a back room. While he counts out the money, she smirks. "You're a little feisty thing, Jada. Those pills still working out for you?"

I can feel my stomach sink.

"They get the job done, that's for sure." I wink.

Moments later, Juan returns with my payout. He counts it once more before handing it over. I check it in good faith before putting the money into my purse.

Zee stands. "As always, it's a pleasure doing business with you. Take care of yourself out there. I'll have those items for you as soon as I can."

"I sure will," I say, standing to hug her before excusing myself.

Money in hand, I quickly hop back into my car and rev up the engine. I try to contain my excitement, but deep down, I feel that I'm closer than ever to leaving this world behind, which is reassuring, given that I believe that my window to get out of this lifestyle is rapidly closing.

Suddenly, my phone rings, and a new message comes through.

Unknown:

Hi, it's Zayn. We met the other night. How's your leg?

Me:

All healed. Thank you for checking on me.

Zayn:

I'd love to see you again if you're free. Dinner tonight at 8 p.m.?

I stare at the message for a moment, contemplating my response. Then, I type my message and send it.

Me:

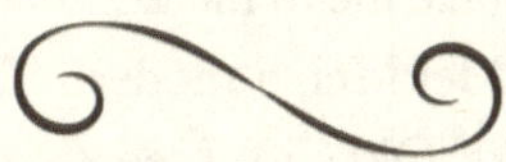

I CAREFULLY EXTEND MY LEG, LATHERING IT WITH VELVETY LOtion. Once my body is moisturized, I stand in front of my full-length mirror for a moment, admiring the way the light catches the curves of my silhouette. I take a deep breath, holding the wine glass in my hand.

Pressing my lips against the brim, I inhale the aromatics before taking a sip. For some reason, my nerves have crept up, which is…different. There's a slight tremble in my hand and a subtle flutter in my chest that I can't quite place. I let out a heavy sigh. I figure a little hint of vanilla in my complex life wouldn't hurt.

My other hand trails down the nape of my neck, over my breasts, then to my stomach before finally landing on my vagina. I lightly rub on my clit and relish the feeling, giving my body permission to relax.

Syd Tha Kyd's voice croons through the speakers, and I lightly sway my hips to the tune for a few moments. I stand there sipping my drink and loosening up. As the song draws to a close, I check the time, and I only have about thirty minutes to get dressed and meet Zayn at the spot. Once my hair is done, I reach over, grabbing my favorite perfume off the vanity table. Leaning my head back, I spritz the elegant yet spicy fragrance at the nape of my neck and then my wrists. Then I walk to my double boudoir closet and step inside, finally settling on a form-fitting black dress that reaches just below my knees. After I slip it on, I step into my patent leather stilettos and out into the night.

Outside, a few moments pass before I wave down a taxi and instruct him to take me to the destination. When my driver pulls in front of Mei Mei, a modern Taiwanese restaurant nestled in the heart of Old City, I see Zayn looking delectable, holding long white stem roses. When he sees me, he instantly helps me get out of the car.

He hands me the flowers, and I smile, completely surprised, "Thank you, they're gorgeous."

Zayn winks. "You're very welcome."

He guides me inside the restaurant, and we're greeted by a pretty hostess who promptly leads us to our table.

"You look stunning," he whispers into my ear as he places his hand on the small of my back, making my skin hot.

The ambiance is sexy, the decor giving odes to beautifully painted Geishas that cover its walls, the ceilings adorned with elegant chandeliers and florals complimented by hues of pink and purple lights. At our table, he pulls out the seat for me, and I slide in, "Thank you," I say.

Twenty minutes later, we're enjoying our first round of cocktails and appetizers, which is an impressive spread of shrimp tempura, edamame, and expertly prepared dumplings.

"Wait, so you were a B2K fan girl? Say it isn't so." He chuckles, resting his chin on his fingers, his sculpted muscles pressing through his shirt.

"Hey, don't judge me, they were it," I say, slightly embarrassed by my confession.

We both laugh, eager to take some of the heat off me. I take a final sip of my cocktail and then place it down, staring intently into his dark brown eyes. "Now it's your turn. What's your story, Zayn?"

He licks his lips, amused by my brashness. "Well, Stormy, I'm originally from West Philly, but I guess you can say that I moved around a lot. It was just me and my mom, and I got in trouble quite a bit, so she moved to try and better my surroundings. I didn't know my father and was pretty pissed off about it. I managed to get my shit together in high school and eventually went to college. By my junior year, my mother got sick and suddenly passed away. I joined the military to cope, I guess. I didn't connect with my dad until much later in life, that is, until he died within a few years after. Since then, I've lived in twelve countries, and I'm currently deciding whether I want to set up in Dubai or Nigeria for the next few months."

"So, the world is your playground? You sure lucked out."

"I own and operate one of the top security technology companies in the country. I guess you can say it requires me to travel quite a bit," he says.

Just then, as the waitress returns with our entrées, Zayn orders us another round of drinks. When she disappears, I'm eager to dive back into our conversation.

"What brought you back to Philly?" I ask.

He shrugs, leaning forward. "I guess you can say that I'm still drawn to its grungy charm."

We share a lighthearted laugh and proceed to dive into our food. My crispy fried snapper is skillfully cooked and seasoned with just enough spice to warm my skin. After a few moments, the waitress returns with more cocktails and sets them down before excusing herself once more.

When she does, Zayn asks, "What about you? Tell me something interesting."

I swallow my food, unsure of how to answer. Although I was enjoying myself, I wasn't quite sure if I was ready to reveal my truth, I don't normally open up like this, especially to men, but with Zayn, I feel a certain ease that is foreign to me.

I hold my hand up to my mouth and slightly cough to clear my throat. "Well, I grew up in foster care."

His eyes instantly become apologetic, and he reaches his hand to touch mine. "I'm sorry."

"Don't be, I'm not," I say.

Zayn smiles, seemingly impressed by my confession. He picks up his glass, offering a toast. "Here's to not letting our pasts define us."

"Cheers to that." We tap our glasses.

A little while later, we step out of Mei Mei, feeling tipsy and full of laughter. I wave my hand, attempting to grab a cab.

"Why don't you let me take you home?" Zayn asks, his hand gently holding mine.

"Are you sure?"

He nods. "I insist. I have a driver. Trust me, it's no trouble at all."

In one smooth motion, he offers me his arm, and I loop mine into his. We cross the street, approaching the black Chevy Tahoe that awaits, and as we do, the driver gets out.

"Stormy, this is Eris," Zayn says.

Eris nods. "It's a pleasure to meet you, miss."

I smile. "Thank you."

Eris opens the door for us, and Zayn helps me inside before sliding into the seat himself, "Where to sir?"

Zayn looks at me, waiting for a response.

"17th and Race," I say, then I turn to Zayn, still high on our playful banter. "So, what do you have planned for the rest of the night? Formulating a plan to infiltrate foreign enemies?"

Zayn chuckles, revealing his perfectly white teeth and chiseled jawline. "Perhaps."

We spend the short ride in comfortable silence, his hand gently resting on my lower thigh. There's something about his touch that feels… natural, easy.

As I stare out of the tinted windows, watching the streetlights and skyscrapers blur by, I feel a strange sense of calm washing over me. Usually, I'm on guard, calculating every move, but right now, with him, it's different. There's a magnetic pull, an undeniable attraction, like a moth to a flame.

I know he's got money—everything about him exudes wealth and power. Maybe, just maybe, he could be another sponsor, someone to add to my list. But something in me hesitates. I'm not quite sure yet if I want to go down that path with him.

Before I know it, we're pulling up in front of my apartment building. I hesitate to get out, a wave of disappointment washing over me as I realize I'm not ready for the night to come to an end. There's a part of me that wants to invite him up to see where this connection could lead, but another part that's cautious and wary of getting too close too soon.

I grip my roses and place my hand on the door, carefully considering my next words. "Would you like to come in?"

He grins a smile that makes me want to melt. "Absolutely."

Back inside my place, I take our coats and hang them up as Zayn walks around, admiring my home.

"Would you like some wine?" I call out as I head to the kitchen.

"Sure," he says.

I grab some glasses and then reach into my wine fridge and pull out a bottle of Merlot. Just as I am about to open the bottle up, he steps into the kitchen, joining me. "Your place is really nice. That view is incredible. Here, let me get that for you."

He takes the bottle from me, opening it with ease.

"Thank you," I say as I begin pouring our glasses.

When I pass him his glass, he stares at me for a moment. I can tell that he's carefully contemplating his next words, "I like you."

I sip my wine nervously. "I like you too."

"Can I kiss you? I've got to admit, I've been wanting to do so all night," he says.

His confidence is such a turn-on. I smile and slowly nod my head yes. Zayn takes a sip of his wine, places the glass down on the countertop, and then approaches me. He gently places his hands on the sides of my neck, leaning down to kiss me.

Without warning, I get lost in his kiss, pressing my chest against his as his tongue explores mine. His hands travel down, gripping my ass, and I feel a familiar warmth spreading through my thighs. My body responds instinctively, a surge of desire that's hard to ignore. But then, something inside me shifts—a flicker of fear, of vulnerability.

This isn't like the other times. I'm used to putting on a show because it's a means to an end. But this—liking someone, being genuinely attracted to them just because—feels different. Deep down, I know that I will soon be leaving this all behind. Perhaps that's why I feel that I can let my guard down for once. But still, it's unsettling, and the ease with which I'm falling into it scares me.

Suddenly, my instincts kick in, and I quickly push him away, fighting against the pull of my urges. I can't let myself get swept up in this, not when I'm so used to being in control, to keeping my emotions in check. This feels too real, too raw, and I'm not sure I'm ready for what that means.

"I'm sorry, this is way too fast," I say.

We both stand there. Seconds feel like minutes, our chests heaving from the attraction. For the next few moments, I try my hardest to fight my desires. I walk into the living room, kick off my heels, and take a seat on my couch. Staring out into the night sky, I try to distract myself from the lustful yearning growing within. But when he sits down beside me and places his arm around my shoulder, I completely fail, pulling him in for another kiss.

I climb on top of his lap to straddle him, wrapping my arms around his neck. As I do, I feel his strong hands grip my waist, pulling my body closer to his. Our lips become lost in one another, my body aching with hunger for him. The touch of his skin, his smell, is completely intoxicating to me. As if my body is already accustomed to his essence. I hike up my dress, grinding myself into his hard dick that is now poking through his pants.

Eager to feel him, I pull away to tug off his shirt. He follows by using his fingers to unzip my dress, the two of us never taking our sights off each other. I pull my arms out of the sleeves of my dress and then undo my bra, exposing my breasts.

"You're so beautiful," he says between kisses.

I gasp as his tongue trails my neck and down to my nipples. I bite my lip and toss my head back, grinding into him once more. His mouth is hot and insistent, and I shiver with pleasure as his hands travel over my body, exploring every inch of my skin.

He pulls me even closer, his hands slipping under my dress to grasp my bare thighs. The feel of his fingers on my skin sends shivers down my spine. His touch is both gentle and demanding, making my pulse quicken with anticipation.

I arch my back, pressing my breasts into his mouth as he kisses and sucks, his tongue flicking over my sensitive nipples. The sensation is overwhelming, and I let out a moan of pure pleasure.

Unable to resist any longer, I reach between us and unbutton his pants, freeing his erection. His hands move to help me, and in a matter of moments, we are both stripped of our clothes, our bodies pressed together in a fevered embrace.

He lifts me effortlessly, and I feel him slip on a condom and position himself at my entrance. Our eyes lock, and for a moment, time stands still. Then, with a slow, powerful thrust, he fills me completely. I cry out, the intensity of the moment overwhelming.

We move together, our bodies finding a rhythm that is both urgent and exquisite. Each movement, each touch, brings us closer to the edge. His hands grip my hips, guiding me as I ride him, my nails digging into his shoulders as I lose myself in the sensation.

"Damn, you feel so good," he groans, his voice thick with desire.

I can only respond with another moan, my body trembling with pleasure. The intensity of our connection is almost too much to bear, and I feel the pressure building within me, ready to explode.

As we move faster, our breaths become ragged, our movements more frantic. The room is filled with the sounds of our lovemaking, a symphony of passion and desire. I can feel the climax building, and I know he is close, too.

With one final thrust, we both reach our peak, our bodies shuddering in unison. The world fades away, leaving only the sensation of him inside me, the warmth of his body against mine, and the overwhelming pleasure of our release.

Together, we collapse, our bodies covered in a sweet mist of sweat. Breathless and spent, we hold each other tightly. As his arm wraps around my waist, I allow the sense of contentment and satisfaction to creep in, even if it's only for one evening. The dark sky outside the window seems brighter, the stars shining more brilliantly than ever before.

CHAPTER

Nine

BENEATH THE SURFACE

Tempest

"Everyone, close your eyes, take a deep breath, and clear your mind," my yoga instructor's voice guides us.

The soft sounds of waves crashing play through the speakers, transporting our minds to a serene beach.

"Now, let your body lay heavy on the floor beneath you. Allow yourself to breathe and become one with the universe," she continues.

I inhale deeply, filling my lungs with as much air as possible before slowly exhaling through my mouth. I focus on my breath, trying to clear my thoughts. More waves crash, the noise of wading water distracting me.

Did I turn off my coffee pot?

I squeeze my eyes shut tighter. According to Fatima, yoga is supposed to be relaxing, but I haven't been able to achieve anything remotely close to it.

The tip of my nose itches, pulling me back to reality and out of my thoughts for a brief moment. I try my best to let it pass and ease back into my focused breathing. Just as I do, a soft bell rings out in the cozy space.

The instructor says, "Now, take one deep, cleansing breath and sigh out."

I do as I'm told, letting my breath go with the rest of the class.

"Open your eyes and come to a seated position," she says from the head of the room. Her long locs are pulled into a neat ponytail, and a playful ring decorates her nose.

My classmates and I follow suit, coming up to a seated lotus pose.

"Take one more cleansing breath and breathe out," she instructs.

In unison, we do this, sighing, "Om."

Placing both hands together in front of her heart and bowing her head, we mimic her movements. "Namaste."

She smiles, her lilac yoga set radiating against her espresso-hued skin. "Thanks for joining us today. Once again, my name is Nova, and it's been a pleasure to share this space with you."

As class is dismissed, I roll up my yoga mat and gather my things, eager to head home. I'd only agreed to attend this class because Fatima begged me to. Unfortunately, she called this morning in quite a jam, needing to reschedule. Despite the sudden change of plans and my best judgment, I decided to come anyway.

"Hi, Tempest, right?"

I look up to see my instructor, Nova, smiling at me.

"Hi, yes, that's me," I reply.

She asks, "How did you enjoy class?"

"I liked it. I didn't realize how hard it would be to relax," I confess.

Nova nods, "Trust me, I get it. It took me almost a year of practice before I could meditate for more than an hour."

"An hour? And here I am complaining about ten minutes."

"It was five," she says.

We both laugh.

"A few of us are going to stop by the café across the street. Would you like to join?" she asks, a friendly gesture.

I lie, "I'd love to, but I actually have to get to work."

"Okay, well, enjoy your Sunday," she says before turning to greet her other students.

As she does, I put on my parka coat, expertly zip it up, and throw my yoga mat over my shoulder. Stepping outside, I'm greeted by small, powdery snowflakes that gently coat the street and cars, adding a serene beauty to the cityscape. The cold air is refreshing, a crisp contrast to the warmth of the studio, and I take a deep breath, savoring the quiet moment.

But as I walk toward my car, something—or rather someone—catches my eye. My heart skips a beat when I see Lance walking down the street, hand in hand with a woman. My steps falter as I take in the sight, the easy way they move together, the familiarity in their gestures.

She's beautiful—effortlessly so. Her skin is a warm, rich walnut, and she's rocking a full, gorgeous fro that frames her face like a halo. She's stylish, too, dressed in a chic winter coat that complements her figure perfectly. There's an undeniable grace in the way she walks beside Lance, like they're perfectly in sync.

Then, as they pass by an antique shop, I notice the glint of a ring on her finger—an engagement ring. The realization hits me like a punch to the gut, leaving me momentarily breathless. I stand frozen, the snowflakes falling around me, my heart pounding in my chest as I watch them walk away, completely oblivious to my presence.

It's a stark reminder of everything I've lost, of how much things have changed. I thought I was moving on, that I was healing, but seeing Lance like this... it brings all the pain rushing back, sharper than ever.

I force myself to keep walking, to reach my car, but the image of them together, of that ring, is seared into my mind, a bitter reminder that some wounds take longer to heal than others.

THIRTY MINUTES LATER, I ASCEND THE STEPS TO FATIMA'S SLEEK two-bedroom townhome and ring the doorbell. As I wait, the snow flurries have intensified, an unexpected prelude to the holiday season. Despite the chill, there's a certain charm to the early and unexpected snowfall, a fleeting reminder of the whimsy of winter. But my mind is elsewhere—still reeling from the sight of Lance with that woman, her engagement ring glinting under the streetlight. The image plays over and over in my head, like a wound that keeps reopening.

Moments later, Fatima swings open the door, her hair wrapped in a colorful scarf, dressed in cozy sweats, with a hint of exhaustion in her eyes.

"Hey, girl! I wasn't expecting you," Fatima greets me, ushering me inside her home.

I force a smile, giving her a brief hug. The space reflects her eclectic taste and vibrant personality—a fusion of modern elegance and inviting warmth. Soft cream and blush tones harmonize with bold, eccentric art pieces, creating a captivating ambiance.

Midnight, her Scottish Fold cat, pads into the foyer, his dense slate-gray fur brushing against her legs in greeting.

Handing over the food, I inquire, "You sounded a bit frantic in your voicemail, so I thought I'd check in. Everything okay?"

Inspecting the bag, she exclaims, "You're the best! Is this from our favorite spot?"

I smirk, slipping out of my boots. "Girl, you know it is."

Fatima's face lights up. "Make yourself at home. I'll grab some plates."

I settle onto her plush, cream-colored sectional, adorned with an array of patterned and textured throw pillows in vibrant hues. As I sink into the softness, my mind races, unable to shake the image of Lance and his fiancée. The unsettled feelings eat away at me, but I decide to keep them to myself. I'm tired of being the one who always brings gloom into our conversations. Fatima has been my rock through so much, and I don't want to burden her with more of my woes—especially not today.

Absentmindedly, I peruse the stack of fashion and lifestyle magazines on the coffee table, accompanied by a vase of fresh flowers. Midnight hops onto the soft arm of the couch, keeping a watchful eye on my movements.

But the guilt lingers, heavy and persistent. I wish I could just let it all out and share my pain with someone who would understand, but for now, I decide to keep my turmoil tucked away, buried beneath the surface where it can't hurt anyone else.

In the midst of bustling in the kitchen, Fatima calls out, "Sorry about ditching you earlier. I've been buried in this article; you know how it goes."

Flipping through the pages of Essence magazine, I counter, "Too well. You're a writing machine."

Fatima chuckles, joining me with a spread of our favorite dishes—pad Thai, chicken satay, and green curry. "The senior editor has been breathing down my neck about that article I mentioned."

I take a bite of my grilled chicken, nodding sympathetically. "Sounds hectic. Did you manage to finish it?"

Seating herself beside me, Fatima nods. "Thankfully, yes. Just finished all the edits and hit send before you arrived. Fingers crossed it goes smoothly."

"I'm sure it's brilliant," I reassure her, savoring the flavors.

She blushes slightly, then adds, "I'm just ready to step out on my own, you know? I'm so sick of the corporate politics. I think it's time to do my own thing, create a platform to tell our stories."

I playfully pat her leg. "That's dope, Fatima. If anyone can do that, it's you!"

She smiles, a mix of excitement and nervousness in her eyes. "I think that I'm finally ready to take the leap. It's scary, but I think it's time."

"Well, when you do, make sure to send me your first publication," I say.

"You know I got you, girl." She winks.

"So, about this article, you really think someone is targeting these men?" I inquire, my curiosity piqued.

She nods emphatically. "Absolutely. I've managed to secure a rather trustworthy source."

My brow furrows. "A source, huh. And who exactly are they suggesting is responsible?"

Fatima's eyes light up. "Their wives."

Silence descends upon the room as I chew on my chicken, contemplating this revelation.

"How was yoga? Nova's a gem, isn't she?" Fatima inquires, changing the subject.

"I felt a little awkward at first, but it was actually refreshing. And yes, Nova was great," I reply. "She invited me to grab coffee after class."

Fatima's eyes sparkle mischievously. "She invited you for coffee afterward? Sounds like someone's got a crush."

My cheeks flush at the implication. "What? No way."

Fatima laughs, her tone teasing, "Trust me, girl, I know these things."

THE NEXT MORNING, I TAKE MY TIME GETTING READY FOR THE day. Settling on a pair of casual slacks and a turtleneck, I pull my long braids back into a low ponytail. I glance out my bedroom window, noticing the snow from the previous day has magically melted away overnight. Reaching for my Glock 19 gun and holster on the bedside table, I carefully secure them in place.

I arrive at the police precinct thirty minutes later, ready to tackle the day's tasks. But the frustration gnaws at me—despite all my digging, there's not much to support my theory that Clay Winthrop was murdered because of his dirty dealings. It feels like I'm back at square one, chasing shadows instead of answers.

At my desk, I settle into my seat, power up my computer, and arrange my workspace, trying to push down the irritation bubbling inside me. Just as I start to get into the rhythm of my morning routine, Maldonado walks in, her energy as upbeat as ever, but today, it's just another reminder of how far I still have to go.

"Good morning, Detective," she greets me.

"Good morning," I reply, looking up.

She smiles and hands me a coffee. "I took a guess—vanilla latte?"

"Thank you, Maldonado. This is very nice of you," I say, surprised by her kindness.

"It's no problem at all," she says, removing her coat. "Did you do anything fun this weekend?"

I take a sip and nod. "Actually, I tried yoga for the first time."

"That's awesome."

"How about you?" I ask, surprising myself. Normally, I have a low tolerance for small talk, but Maldonado is growing on me.

She takes notice of my unusual interest and says with excitement. "Me? I went to check out the Sixers game with some friends. It was really fun."

At that moment, McGregor strides over, his arrogance emanating like a noxious cloud. "Maldonado, are you available? I need your assistance on the Jane Doe case."

I detect the surprise in her expression; she's been eager to immerse herself in real investigative work and, as of late, seemingly put to the task. "Sir? I'm currently aiding Detective Blaze on her case."

"Not anymore, you're not," McGregor asserts, then shifts his attention to me. "I trust you can handle a minor case on your own, Blaze. After all, you're Sterling's star pupil. There's nothing you can't handle, am I right?"

I maintain my composure. "I've got it under control."

Without so much as a glance back at Maldonado, McGregor states, "Let's go, D-one," and strides off toward his office.

Maldonado shoots me a sympathetic look, but I offer her a reassuring smile. She gathers her pen, notebook, and laptop, practically hurrying to join McGregor. I scoff quietly to myself and return my focus to the computer, opening my emails. At the top of my inbox lies a message titled "C. Winthrop Toxicology Report."

I eagerly open it, reading through the details. The report indicates the presence of diazepam and diphenhydramine, although both relatively low, as though he'd taken a sleeping pill of some sort. What catches my attention is the elevated levels of digoxin in Clay's system. I quickly cross-referenced Clay's medical records and found no accounts or family history of heart conditions. So, what could explain having this drug, which is used to treat heart conditions, in his system? Crossing my fingers, I lean in, staring at my computer in an attempt to better process my thoughts.

Suddenly, the realization sets in. What if Clay Winthrop was poisoned?

CHAPTER
Ten

DEVIOUS DEEDS

Stormy

The morning air is comforting, signaling the start of a perfect autumn day. I keep my breath steady as I run along the Delaware River. Dawn has just broken, and bright sunrays peek over the clouds. Ahead, the path is much emptier compared to the warmer summer months, and I much prefer it this way. Honestly, I'd love to have this place all to myself, but I don't mind passing the occasional runner or biker.

When I am done, I take a seat on an empty bench. Looking out onto the river, I'm greeted by the buildings in neighboring Camden, New Jersey. Gentrification is indeed a bitch. I remember when there was nothing but vacant lots and drug dealers that occupied that place. Now, it's filled with luxury apartments and stadiums. A few feet away, a homeless man sleeping on another bench shifts and tugs on his wrangled coat.

I pull out my phone and surf the net, wondering if there are any updates on Clay's death. Using my fingers, I type his name and see his death has been ruled an overdose. "Real Estate Mogul Dies from Heart Attack," the headline reads.

My mind races with confusion. I've been slipping my johns a sleep-inducing remedy for quite some time, and none of them ever had any complications, let alone died on me with the drugs that I use. I reach into my pocket, pulling out the vial Quinn gave me the night we met up at the Navy Yard. I can't seem to forget her insistence about administering this to her husband. Which is exactly why I didn't. Unless I got these drugs mixed up with my own stash that night. Is it possible that I inadvertently played into her hand and killed her husband, and the effects just took a little longer to hit?

No, no, there's simply no way. I would never be that careless or stupid. After all, he was very much asleep and alive when I left that man in his hotel room, as far as I can remember. Deep down, I can't shake the nagging feeling that I'm not quite as sure as I once was. Suddenly, a slight chill crawls over my skin. It dawns on me that I might've gotten myself involved in much more than an idiotic lover's spat.

Later that day, I slide into the booth at my favorite upscale café, the kind of place where chandeliers sparkle even in daylight, and the clink of fine china is music to the ears. Paige is already there, sipping a mimosa, her manicured nails tapping impatiently against the glass. Something she does when she's grown impatient.

"You're late," she says, her tone light, but I catch the irritation simmering just beneath the surface.

"Traffic," I reply, slipping off my sunglasses and flashing a smile, the one that usually smooths things over. "But I'm here now."

She forces a smile, but it doesn't quite reach her eyes. "You always seem to make an entrance."

I shrug it off and reach for the menu. Before I can even glance at it, I notice a group of businessmen at a nearby table giving us the once-over. One of them, tall and sharp in a suit, offers a friendly nod in our direction. I barely pay them any mind, but I can feel Paige stiffen beside me.

The tension in the air is almost palpable. I try to move the conversation along, focusing on the menu, but something's off. I can sense it in the way Paige is watching me.

"You know," she begins, her words slicing through the air, "it's not always about being the center of attention, Stormy. Sometimes, it's about knowing when to blend in, when to let someone else take the spotlight."

I look up, surprised by the sudden shift in her tone. "Where's this coming from?"

She leans back in her seat, her eyes locking onto mine with an intensity that sends a chill down my spine. "Just an observation. It's easy to be the one everyone flocks to, but it's not as easy to keep them once they see past the charm."

Jealousy. It's written all over her face, in the tightness of her lips, in the coldness of her gaze. I force a laugh, trying to brush it off. "I guess we can't all be the quiet, mysterious type like you."

Her smile returns, but it's nothing more than a mask hiding something darker beneath. "No, we can't. But mystery has its advantages. People don't see you coming until it's too late."

There's something in her words, something that makes my skin crawl. But I play along, not wanting to give her the satisfaction of knowing she's gotten under my skin. "Maybe, but charm has its perks too."

We move on, chatting about the usual—life and plans for the weekend. Just as we're about to wrap up, my phone buzzes with a text from Paige. It's an invitation. I look up to see her smiling at me from across the table.

"I hope you're free Thursday night," she says.

"Thursday? I should be. What's up?" I ask.

"I'm hosting my first charity event, and I want you there," she announces, her excitement clear. "It's time you meet a husband so that you can retire your cat burglar days, girl."

"Um, I don't know," I say. All I want to do right now is keep a low profile, which, according to her assessment, I'm not doing too good a job of.

"Nope, I refuse to hear otherwise," she says.

That evening, sprawled across my couch, I stare at my bank account, contemplating my next move. As it turns out, I have more than enough money to leave and start anew. I look up plane tickets to Paris, Portugal, and Ghana, eager to settle on a destination. I could book a one-way ticket right now and leave Philly and all this drama behind.

Minutes pass as I weigh my options: see this whole Clay mess through and keep my ears to the street, or leave before any trouble comes my way.

When my cell rings, I smile at Zayn's name on the screen. "Hello?" I answer.

"You sound even sexier over the phone. I like it," he says, flirting.

I blush. "Is that so? Like a sexy call girl?"

"Way better than that," Zayn replies. "I want to see you again. Are you free tonight?"

I rise from my couch, slowly pacing through my living room. "I don't know. I guess it depends."

"On?"

I suddenly feel myself become nervous. "On what you had in mind," I say.

Zayn remains cool. "How about I come over and cook you some dinner?"

"You cook too? Is there anything you can't do?" I say, teasing him.

He giggles. "I can't share all my secrets too soon."

"Is that so? Hmm, I may need to reconsider," I challenge.

"How about this, over dinner, I'll tell you everything you need to know," he offers.

"Sounds like a deal to me," I say.

I can hear him smile through the phone. "Good, I'll see you soon."

When we hang up, I try to let the butterflies in my belly settle. He is absolutely electrifying, yet mysterious and a little naughty; I can't exactly put my hand on it. I look down at my baggy sweats and regret spending the rest of the day on my couch being a complete slob. I check the time, and hurry into the bathroom.

An hour later, I walk through my place, making sure everything is tidy and presentable. The night sky has fallen, and the moon, full and bright, shines through my apartment. I turn on some soft tunes and light a fragrant candle. Moments later, I hear a soft knock at the door. My palms grow slightly sweaty as I make my way toward my entrance. I take one last glance at myself in the mirror, hoping the lounge dress that hugs my body doesn't come off as an act of desperation. This nervousness is so foreign to me, causing my mind to race and fill with thoughts of panic and excitement.

When I open the door and lay my eyes on him, those thoughts evaporate. Standing here before me, he looks much better than I remembered, which seems impossible. Holding a grocery bag styled in casual jeans, a gray T-shirt, and a bomber coat, I let him in. When he steps into the confines of my apartment, he gives me a warm, comforting hug.

"You look nice," he compliments.

I smile. "Thank you."

Leading him into the kitchen, I take his coat. "The pots and pans are over there. Is there anything I can help you with?"

Zayn smiles. "How about you pour us some wine and take a seat."

I'm immediately impressed by his confidence. I do as I'm told, opening a bottle of Sauvignon Blanc, pouring each of us a glass, and taking a seat. "Can I at least know what's for dinner?"

"Butter-poached lobster tails and risotto," he explains as he carefully sets the ingredients on the countertop.

My eyebrow perches. "You do that?"

He nods, clearly amused by my astonishment. "Do you cook?"

I quickly shake my head. "Only toast."

We both laugh this time. While he cooks, we take this moment to get to know each other better. He reveals that he had an older half-brother, the two sharing different mothers. His favorite pastime is playing Spanish guitar, a skill he picked up while living in Barcelona. I share some of my favorite movies and actresses that I watched while growing up and my enjoyment of boxing.

Once dinner is ready, we set up in my living room, more casual and comfortable than I'd ever been with a man in quite some time. I use my fork and bring a small mouthful of the expertly prepared meal to my mouth; the first bite is magnificent.

He watches my reaction carefully. "How'd you like it?"

With my hand covering my lips, I savor the delectable taste on my tongue before swallowing. "Absolutely delicious, truly. I had no idea you were a world-class chef, too!"

Zayn smiles, flattered by my approval. "Only when I think it's worth it."

After dinner, as the credits roll on an episode of *Insecure*, our laughter slowly fades into a comfortable silence. The warmth of the wine and the coziness of the couch create an intimate atmosphere. I find myself further drawn to Zayn's presence beside me and rest my head on his shoulder for a moment.

I don't understand it. I've perfected the art of detachment, of not giving a damn about the men I'm with. They're just transactions, temporary distractions, not real connections. But Zayn... he's different, I'm different. There's this crazy, magnetic pull he has over me, something I can't explain.

I'm used to playing a role, putting on a mask, and keeping my guard up. But with Zayn, I feel my defenses slipping, crumbling with every passing moment. I don't know if I want to stop it or if I even can. This crazy pull, this unexplainable attraction... it's pushing me closer to him, making me want things I'd once sworn off, making me crave something real, something raw, something new.

"Now what?" Zayn asks, interrupting my thoughts.

Feeling a surge of boldness, I lean in and press my lips against his, the taste of the wine lingering between us. His response is immediate, his mouth moving eagerly against mine as our tongues dance in a passionate tango. The kiss deepens, igniting a fire within me that I can't ignore.

His fingers trace the curve of my collarbone, his touch leaving a trail of heat in its wake. I can feel the tension between us, thick and palpable, as he leans in, his lips finding the sensitive skin of my neck.

I tilt my head back, giving him better access as he kisses his way down my throat, his hands busy exploring every inch of exposed skin. With a gentle touch, Zayn lifts me into his arms, carrying me effortlessly toward my bedroom. The anticipation sends shivers down my spine as he lays me down on the soft sheets, his hands moving with purpose as he begins to undress me.

Each article of clothing falls away, leaving me bare and exposed before him. His gaze is intense, filled with desire and adoration as he takes in every inch of my body. I feel vulnerable yet empowered under his scrutiny, my heart pounding with excitement.

Zayn's touch is electric as he explores my skin with his fingertips, sending waves of pleasure coursing through me. I take his index finger into my mouth, sucking slowly, my tongue swirling around it. His eyes darken with lust as I release him, and he slides his now-wet finger between my thighs and then inside me. I lean into him, craving more of his touch as he uses his fingers to stroke me with a feather-light caress that leaves me breathless.

As I lay on my back, Zayn joins me in bed, his body pressed firmly against mine in a heated embrace. His tongue slides down my body with a slow, deliberate intensity, his lips traces a path from my breasts to my most intimate parts that leaves me trembling in anticipation. The first brush of his tongue against my sensitive flesh sends a jolt of pleasure through me, forcing a gasp to escape. I bite down on my lower lip, the sensation overwhelming as I thread my fingers through his hair, pulling him closer.

His mouth works wonders on me, each lick and suck drawing out the most primal of responses. I can feel the tension building, coiling tight within me, until I'm nothing more than a bundle of raw nerves and heightened senses. Zayn devours me; his tongue is relentless as he drinks in every drop of my essence, pushing me closer and closer to the edge.

And then it happens—my body shatters under the force of my climax, waves of pleasure crashing over me in an unstoppable tide. I arch my back, crying out his name as I lose myself completely in the sensation, my mind blank with bliss.

Pleased with my response, Zayn climbs back up my body, his lips capturing mine in a searing kiss. The taste of my nectar on his tongue only fuels the fire raging between us. I open myself to him fully, surrendering to the passion that blazes between us, allowing him to fill me up with every inch of his hard length.

The room is filled with the sound of our ragged breaths and the soft rustle of the sheets as we move together in a frenzied rhythm, each thrust driving us closer to the precipice of ecstasy. The connection between us is undeniable, each touch, each movement, fanning the flames until we're both consumed by the intensity of our need.

When we finally reach the peak, it's explosive—our bodies shuddering together in a symphony of pleasure, the world around us fading away until there's nothing left but the two of us, locked in the throes of passion.

In the aftermath of our lovemaking, we lay entwined in each other's arms, our bodies still buzzing with the aftershocks of pleasure. It's a feeling unlike any other, one that leaves me breathless, one that I never want to end.

CHAPTER
Eleven

ENTANGLEMENTS

Tempest

My morning begins with a stop at Peddler Coffee. As I wait in line to place my order for my usual brown sugar and vanilla latte, my phone buzzes with a text from Fatima.

Fatima:

As promised. Hope you like it.

Intrigued, I click the link to the not-yet-published version of her much-anticipated article. My eyes scan the screen, each word pulling me deeper into the exposé. Fatima's piece uncovers a supposed syndicate of women who've murdered their husbands and seemingly got away with it until now.

Although no names are released, it's quite clear that this circle is very powerful and entrenched within our community. The patterns are obvious: each woman was married to a wealthy man, and every few months, one of these men met an untimely and mysterious death.

Very much like Clay Winthrop.

The realization nearly knocks the wind out of me. When I'm greeted by the barista, I quickly shove my phone into my coat pocket and place my order, still reeling from the uncanny news. The implications of Fatima's article swirl in my mind, a mix of shock and determination settling over me as I try to process the gravity of what I've just read.

An hour later, I quickly review my notes, carefully ensuring all my key points are ready. For some reason, I am very nervous. It's been a lot getting back into the swing of things. And although the help is needed, I won't lie and say I've always felt welcome. I place my pen cap into my mouth, a nervous and disgusting habit that I picked up in my teens. When I check the time, it's less than five minutes to the hour.

Beside me, Maldonado is wrapping up her phone call with a potential witness in her case with McGregor. I take a deep breath and rise from my seat.

As I do, Maldonado hangs up the phone and looks at me. "Ready?"

I nod, my heart racing. "As ready as I'll ever be."

She grabs her notepad and pen and rises to join me, and we take the short walk into the conference chambers. Multiple screens display our unit's current stats, and by the looks of it, they don't look too good.

Maldonado and I find two sets of seats toward the back. We quickly slide into our chairs, eager to get situated before the briefing starts. Moments later, Sergeant Sterling barges in, looking distressed, a look I've grown quite accustomed to in my time back.

He goes to the front of the room, holding a stack of papers, and adjusts the mic. As he does, the light chatter in the room dies out, "We're up to our ass in cases. We need to increase our clearance rates. We need results, team."

The room is tense as Sterling continues, "Cook, any updates on your cases?"

Detective Cook rises from his seat. "Yes sir, narrowing in on my suspect in the Holmes Street murder, just have a few loose ends to tie up to bring forth charges."

Sterling nods, seemingly pleased. "Good. Let me know if you need any support."

"Copy that," Cook says before taking a seat.

"McGregor," Sterling calls out. "What updates do you have on the triple murder case?"

McGregor stands. "We're working on some promising leads, I've brought in Detective Maldonado to assist with following up on those."

Sergent Sterling takes down a few notes. "Good. Let me know if you need any additional support."

The meeting continues with my team members providing updates and statuses on their open investigations. By the end of it, I was the only one who wasn't given an opportunity to share my findings.

"All right, everyone, let's get back to work and get some of these damn cases closed," Sterling states.

Before he dismisses the meeting, I shoot up my hand. "Um, sir?"

"What is it, Blaze?"

My chest becomes slightly heavy. "I have an update on the Winthrop case."

With a puckered brow, Sterling says, "Yes, Winthrop died of natural causes. That case is closed, Detective."

"With all due respect, sir, I don't think Clay Winthrop's death was of natural causes at all. I believe he was murdered, sir," I explain.

Sterling looks indifferent, "What did the autopsy report say the cause of death was, Detective?"

"Heart attack, sir."

"Then it was a heart attack." His tone is condescending. "We are drowning in a whirlwind of shit. We need to focus on closing the open ones, not wasting our time trying to disprove the findings of expert medical examiners!" he scolds.

I can hear snickers from my colleagues.

"Roger that, sir," I say, and take my seat. My skin burns with embarrassment and frustration.

When the briefing ends, I quickly head to the bathroom and take a few deep cleansing breaths. I turn on the water in a hurry, eager for the cool water to calm me down.

Back at my desk, I stare blankly at the computer screen in front of me. My phone buzzes, snapping me out of my thoughts. It's Fatima calling. I quickly pick up, knowing she must need someone to talk to after the week she's had.

"Hey, girl," I answer, trying to inject some cheer into my voice despite the exhaustion creeping in.

"Tempest, I'm so over this damn job," Fatima's voice is thick with frustration, almost cracking with disappointment. "I didn't get the promotion. They gave it to some guy who's only been here for a year. A year! Can you believe that?"

I sigh, feeling her pain. "I'm so sorry, Fatima. That's ridiculous. You've put in so much work."

"I know, right? I've done everything they asked, gone above and beyond, and for what? I'm tired of playing it safe, Tempest. I'm done. It's time I take control of my own destiny. I'm going to start my own company and launch my own magazine. I don't need them to validate me."

Her words hang in the air, full of determination and a fire I've rarely heard in her voice. I feel a swell of pride for my friend. "That's exactly what you should do. You have the talent and the vision. You don't need them to tell you how valuable you are. You can do this, Fatima. I know you can."

There's a brief silence on the other end, and I can tell she's processing everything. "You really think so?"

"I know so," I affirm, my voice steady and filled with conviction. "You've got this. And I'll be right here supporting you every step of the way."

She lets out a deep breath, and I can almost hear the weight lifting off her shoulders through the phone. "Thanks, Tempest. I needed to hear that. Listen, I could really use a drink—actually, a few. How about we go out tonight?"

There's a brief pause, and I can sense her regret as soon as the words leave her mouth. "Oh, Tempest, I'm so sorry. That was thoughtless of me."

I offer a small, understanding smile, even though she can't see it, while guilt tugs at my conscience. I haven't really gone out since everything went down, and though I want to be there for her, I know I'm already stretched thin. But I also believe I'm stronger than my addictions—I have to be. "No worries, Fatima. I'd love to, but I'm tied up with work tonight. Rain check? I promise I'll make it up to you."

Fatima's voice softens, understanding laced with disappointment. "Yeah, okay. Just don't take too long, all right?"

"I won't, I promise," I assure her, even though the guilt gnaws at me. "We'll do something real soon."

"All right," she says, the spark returning to her voice. "Later, Temp."

As I hang up, I feel a pang of regret for turning her down, but I know I'll make it up to her. Tonight, I have bigger fish to fry.

BY THE AFTERNOON, I FIND MYSELF PARKED IN FRONT OF THE Winthrop residence. My instincts were certain that Clay Winthrop was murdered. Given the striking similarities and his wife's indifferent disposition, I decide to take a closer look into Mrs. Winthrop.

Moments pass before I see her luxury vehicle pull into her driveway. I swiftly exit my car and approach her when she opens her car door.

She's surprised to see me. "Detective Blaze, I wasn't expecting you," she remarks.

"Mrs. Winthrop, I need you to be honest with me," I begin, my voice cutting through the tense silence of the moment. "I know this must be a difficult time for you, but we need to get to the bottom of what happened to your husband."

Quinn's eyes narrow slightly, a flicker of apprehension crossing her features. "What exactly are you implying, Detective?" she retorts, her voice laced with a hint of defiance.

I press on, "I find it hard to believe that a man like Clay, in seemingly good health, would just drop dead of a heart attack out of nowhere. Especially considering the circumstances surrounding his death."

Her facade falters with my statement, a brief moment of vulnerability slipping through her carefully crafted mask. "Are you interrogating me?" she counters, her tone laced with a mixture of irritation and uncertainty.

Folding my arms across my chest, I keep my voice low and steady. "I'm simply trying to piece together the facts, Mrs. Winthrop. And right now, it seems like you're hiding something."

With a clenched jaw, she shoots back, "I have nothing to hide. And if you continue with these baseless accusations, I'll be forced to involve my lawyer."

I hold her gaze, unfazed by her threat. "By all means, Mrs. Winthrop," I reply evenly. "But just remember, the truth has a way of surfacing, whether we want it to or not."

I smile before excusing myself and walking back to my car. It's clear that I've gotten under her skin. There's more to this case. I just have to prove it.

That evening, I find myself once again stationed outside the Winthrop residence, my eyes peeled for any signs of suspicious activity. Above, the sky displays a captivating tapestry of shadows, casting an aura of mystique and allure upon the scene.

Taking a break from my surveillance, I indulge in a cheeseburger, my hunger barely masking my determination to unearth any potential clues. Suddenly, a blacked-out truck pulls up in front of the estate, and my attention snaps back to the task at hand as Mrs. Winthrop emerges, dressed in a floor-length gown, and is ushered into the vehicle.

Without hesitation, I follow the truck through winding roads and bustling city streets until it pulls up in front of an upscale property in the heart of the city. The doors are manned by valet drivers and security. There appears to be a gala or some high society event taking place, flanked by elegantly dressed attendees.

Exercising caution to avoid detection, I park my car covertly across the street and stay within the darkness. Then, I reach for my camera, using the large lens to zoom in and get a better glimpse at the array of guests. As Mrs. Winthrop steps out of her car, I watch as she enters the foyer of the building, her demeanor filled with tension. My eyes stay alert as I watch each arrival, snapping photos of the various attendees in elegant attire as they continue to step out of sleek cars and make their way into the building.

The air buzzes with excitement, and I can hear faint strains of music and laughter from the rooftop terrace. Pausing for a moment, I look out of my front windshield and up to the sky, following the noise. I slip my hand into my coat pocket to pull out my voice recorder and document my thoughts, wondering what it all could possibly mean. When I finish, I place the device down onto my passenger seat and proceed to capture images. Then, to my astonishment, I spot Jada among the guests, sending a jolt of surprise coursing through me. My mind races with questions, wondering what nasty web my estranged sister could possibly be entangled in.

CHAPTER
Twelve

THE MUSE
Stormy

Paige's penthouse is the epitome of urban luxury, perched atop one of Philadelphia's tallest skyscrapers. The private elevator doors open directly into the expansive living area, where floor-to-ceiling windows frame breathtaking panoramic views of the city skyline, sparkling under the evening sky. I take a deep breath, wearing a stunning floor-length topaz gown that accentuates my figure.

Outside, the rooftop terrace is the centerpiece of the event, elegantly decorated with twinkling fairy lights, exotic potted plants, and conveniently placed heating fixtures, creating an enchanting and welcoming ambiance. Guests mingle, their conversations blending with the soft strains of a live jazz band playing in the background. Waitstaff glides through the crowd, offering trays of gourmet hors d'oeuvres and flutes of champagne.

I take a glass and make my way to the railing, gazing out over the city lights and the life below. Deep down, I feel out of place and silently regret agreeing to attend this event. I sigh and look around, assessing the crowd. The guests are a tapestry of the city's elite, each one seemingly more influential and enigmatic than the last. It's strange—you can practically smell the money in the air. Normally, I'd be excited about events like this, but something feels off. These are the true movers and shakers, the ones who make high-stakes decisions and business deals that trickle down to affect us all. I'm both awestruck and suspicious of how quickly Paige managed to weave her way into this crowd.

Just then, Paige joins us all, radiant in a sleek emerald gown that glimmers against her honey-kissed skin. Under the lights, I watch as she moves through the crowd with practiced grace, greeting each guest personally. Her charm is magnetic, and she effortlessly balances conversations with warmth, elegance, and duty.

As she makes her way over, I notice two women trailing close behind her, clearly part of the inner circle Paige has been cultivating. One of them is a tall, statuesque woman with jet-black hair styled in a sharp bob, her eyes cool and assessing behind cat-eye glasses. She's dressed in a crimson cocktail dress that hugs her curves, exuding confidence and a sense of authority. The other is petite, with caramel-colored skin and a cascade of curls that bounce with every step. Her dress, a shimmering gold number, complements her playful smile, but there's a sharpness in her gaze that tells me she's not just here for the fun of it.

When Paige spots me, she immediately breaks away from the duo to greet me. A genuine smile lights up her face. "Storm, I'm so glad you could make it!" Paige says, her voice filled with excitement. "Isn't this fabulous?"

As she speaks, I catch the two women exchanging a look, their eyes briefly flicking over me before returning to Paige. It's subtle, but there's something in that look—a mixture of curiosity and assessment—that makes me wonder just what Paige has gotten herself into with these women.

"It is," I reply, briefly tearing away from her gaze and through the likes of the party. "You've really outdone yourself with this, girl."

Paige beams. "Thank you. I hope everyone else thinks so."

The two mystery women excuse themselves, conversing with other attendees.

"Since when do you care what these people think?" I ask. Her sudden need for approval among this rank of society has been a surprise, to say the least.

"I don't, just getting in where I fit in," she says.

I nod and take a sip of my champagne. "And these are all Dom's friends? How'd you manage to bring them all out?"

Almost instantly, I can sense her skittishness. "Oh, this charity cause. Don't worry. We'll have plenty of time to get into that later."

My brow perches, curious about her response. But before I can counter, she smiles, tossing her arm around my shoulder, and whispers in my ear, "All you need to worry about is finding yourself a husband. I think you'll find a lot of prospects."

I snort at her statement, and she chuckles. Just then, a hush falls over the crowd as a striking woman steps onto the terrace. She commands attention with every step, exuding an air of power and sophistication. Dressed in a floor-length, midnight-blue gown that shimmers like the night sky, the woman is reminiscent of Vanessa Williams in her prime. Her hair is styled in soft waves that frame her face, and she wears a pair of diamond drop earrings that sparkle like stars. There's no denying that her presence is magnetic, drawing the eyes of everyone in attendance, including mine.

I watch her captivated. She carries herself with a regal poise, acknowledging the respectful nods and whispers with a serene smile. At her side, she is flanked by an impeccably dressed male attendant, who ensures her path is clear, and her comfort is maintained at all times.

"Who is that?" I say, whispering to Paige.

Paige's demeanor shifts slightly, a mixture of admiration and nerves. "Stormy, I'd like you to meet someone very important," she says, guiding me toward the woman. "This is Gabrielle Dubois."

Gabrielle turns to face us, her smile dazzling and eyes sharp, "Paige, Bonjour, ma chère! This event is simply marvelous. I've taught you quite well," she says, her voice smooth and commanding. "And who is this lovely guest?"

Her eyes narrow slightly, and I can feel her assessing my presence with an intensity that makes me feel exposed.

"This is Stormy," Paige introduces, her voice steady but filled with reverence. "She's the woman I was telling you about."

Suddenly, Gabrielle's expression changes. "Is that so?" her tone is laced with intrigue. She then takes my hand, a sense of adoration now in her gaze. "Magnifique! It is a pleasure to meet you, Stormy. Your story is truly inspiring."

"Thank you," I say, although I'm extremely confused by this interaction.

Just then, her silent attendant leans into her ear and whispers something. Gabrielle is then promptly whisked away, leaving Paige and I to resume our conversation.

I quickly turn my attention to Paige. "What was that all about?"

She instantly becomes tense. "What do you mean?"

I can tell she's avoiding my question, but I don't budge. "What did she mean by my story being inspiring?"

There's a lengthy pause before she responds, "I kind of used you as my muse for this event."

"Muse? What do you mean by that?" I inquire.

Her eyes become shifty. "Well, I sort of told Gabrielle about your time in foster care and may have proposed a fundraiser aimed at helping those displaced by parents addicted to drugs."

I nearly choke. "You did what?"

Paige continues, "Look, I'm sorry, I needed something that would make me stand out to her. These women are tough to crack. I found an in, and I used it."

My skin grows hot, "And you needed to do that at my expense?" I can feel my patience wearing thin.

Before Paige can say another word, I promptly excuse myself, rushing off the terrace and back into the penthouse. I feel as though I'm going to be sick. The sound of clinking glasses and soft jazz fades as I search for the bathroom. The opulence of the penthouse is evident in the plush carpets and tasteful artwork adorning the walls.

I continue down a dimly lit hallway, still reeling from my exchange with Paige. As I do, a familiar hushed voice catches my attention from behind a door slightly left open.

"...I can assure you that won't be necessary," Quinn's voice says, irritation clear in her tone. "Everything is under control."

Another voice, smooth and commanding, responds, and I quickly realize it's Gabrielle Dubois. "Under control? We can't afford any more mistakes, Quinn. Not now, with so much at stake."

My pulse quickens as I sense the significance of this conversation. Peeking over my shoulder, I gently nudge the door open just a bit more, careful not to make a sound. The room is a study, richly decorated with dark wood and leather-bound books. Quinn and Gabrielle are standing near a large window overlooking the city, their backs turned toward me.

Quinn sighs, brushing a strand of hair from her face. "I've handled it. They have nothing on me, that I can assure you."

Gabrielle steps closer, her voice dropping to a menacing whisper. "Handled? I don't think you grasp the gravity of the situation, Quinn. Your little games are starting to affect us all."

Quinn's demeanor shifts slightly, her confidence faltering. "Gabrielle, I—"

Before Quinn can finish her sentence, Gabrielle's hand whips across her face with a sharp crack that echoes in the room. Quinn stumbles back, clutching her cheek, her eyes wide with shock and fury.

"Don't think for a second that you're untouchable," Gabrielle hisses, her voice cold and threatening. "You may have fooled others, but I see right through you. And if you jeopardize everything we've worked for, I'll make sure you regret it."

Quinn straightens, her face flushed with anger but something else too—fear. "I won't let you down, Gabrielle. I'll fix this. Just... give me time."

Gabrielle studies her for a moment, her expression unreadable before she finally steps back. "See that you do. This is your last chance."

The tension in the room is thick enough to cut with a knife, and I find myself holding my breath, afraid to make even the slightest noise. My breath catches, a sinking feeling settling in the pit of my stomach as I realize they may be discussing Clay's death. I strain to hear more, but my focus is interrupted by the sound of approaching footsteps. Panic surges through me, and I swiftly pivot, retreating down the corridor and slipping into the nearest open room.

To my surprise, I collide with Gabrielle's attendant, or lover, whom I'm not quite sure. His eyes darken, narrowing with suspicion. Maintaining composure, I muster a casual tone. "Could you point me in the direction of the bathroom?"

In a silent gesture, he points to the right with a single finger. I offer a grateful smile before swiftly excusing myself. Alone in the bathroom, I lock the door and lean against it, attempting to steady my racing breath. The cryptic words from the overheard conversation echo in my mind, sending a shiver down my spine.

As I gather my wits, I decide to leave and head home. This feels like a mistake, like I'm meddling in something I shouldn't be. Stepping back into the hallway, the sounds of laughter from the gala fade into the background as I make my way toward the elevators.

I press the call button and wait, the anticipation building with each passing second. Finally, a soft bell chimes, signaling the arrival of the elevator. But as the double doors slide open, my confusion deepens when I see Zayn standing inside. Our eyes meet in a moment of mutual surprise. Zayn's expression mirrors my own confusion, and then he promptly reaches for my hand, pulling me onto the hoist with him.

He presses the button to close the elevator door, his eyes intense as he turns to me. "Stormy, what are you doing here?"

I meet his gaze, a mixture of surprise and curiosity coursing through me. "What are you doing here?" I counter, the words slipping out before I can stop them, the tension palpable in the confined space of the elevator.

His expression tightens slightly, a flicker of something unreadable crossing his features. "This is my brother's penthouse," he reveals, his voice barely above a whisper.

I feel the blood drain from my face at his revelation. "Your brother is Dominic Hansen?" I stammer, the implications of his connection to Paige hitting me like a ton of bricks.

Zayn nods solemnly. "Half-brother," he clarifies, his eyes holding mine with a mix of concern and understanding.

The weight of his words settles over me like a heavy blanket, the pieces of the puzzle finally falling into place. "That means you're Paige's brother-in-law," I murmur, my mind reeling with the sudden flood of revelations.

He reaches out, his touch gentle as he takes my hand in his. "I know this must be a lot to take in, but please trust me. I'll explain everything later," he assures me, his voice tinged with sincerity.

Before I can respond, the elevator doors slide open, and he guides me outside. Zayn signals to his driver, Eris, who steps forward to escort me out. As we make our way to the waiting car, his urgency becomes more apparent.

"But for now, you need to leave. These women, they're dangerous. You don't want to get mixed up in whatever they're involved in," he warns, his tone grave.

With a final nod, he helps me into the back of the car, his eyes holding mine for a fleeting moment longer before the door closes, and we drive off into the night. As the city lights blur past, I'm left alone with my thoughts, grappling with the unsettling realization that nothing is as it seems.

CHAPTER
Thirteen

ANOTHER COMPLICATION

Tempest

I walk into my vestibule later that night, the weight of the day hanging heavy on my shoulders. As I peel off my jacket and remove my gun, I'm met with a familiar sight: another crack in the tile. Great, one more problem to add to my ever-growing to-do list.

My home, nestled in Wynnewood, is a multi-floor unit left to me as part of my inheritance from my parents. They showered me with love and protection until they died, and I spent much of my life blaming myself for their sudden and tragic passing. It took a long time to accept that I could never have anticipated the chain of events that followed when I insisted we go grab some water ice to combat the hot summer day. None of us could have predicted the drunk driver who crashed into our car head-on. Both of my parents died on impact while I walked away with barely a scratch—a fact that still makes no sense to me to this day.

When I first met Jada, I told her I killed my parents. The truth is, I blamed myself for the accident, and it's a weight I've carried ever since. Even now, it's hard to shake the guilt, no matter how much I try to convince myself otherwise.

I squeeze my eyes shut, burying those thoughts and feelings. That sense of warmth and security their love provided feels like a distant memory. Passing by the makeshift board adorned with photos of my parents, a map of Philadelphia, and reminders of a past that feels both comforting and suffocating, I make my way upstairs.

The day's tension begins to melt away as I step into the shower, letting the hot water cascade over me, washing away the stress and exhaustion. It's a moment of solace in a world filled with chaos and uncertainty. After drying off and slipping into my favorite pajamas, I head to the kitchen to heat up some Chinese take-out. The aroma fills the air, comforting in its familiarity.

While I wait, a whirlwind of thoughts swirls in my mind. Had I connected Quinn Winthrop to the mysterious secret society of wealthy women killing off their husbands? What did Jada have to do with this? I pull out my phone and stare at her contact information, the contemplation of whether I should call her nagging at me. The beep of the microwave sounds off, and I quickly decide against it.

With my plate in hand, I settle onto the couch and start flicking through the channels, hoping to find something to take my mind off things. The TV's glow fills the room as I skim through the usual shows—cooking competitions, home renovation projects, or reruns of "Martin." These little distractions are comforting, offering a break from the constant noise in my head. As I watch, I glance around my place, thinking about what my next home renovation project should be. Fixing up the house has been my focus lately—each crack I repair and each room I redo feels like I'm patching up parts of myself, too.

Knowing that Lance is engaged now—it's like a sucker punch, knocking the wind right out of me. Seeing him with someone else, seeing her wear the ring that should've been mine, brings back all the pain I've been trying to forget.

And then there's Jada. I want to reach out, to warn her, to help her. But how can I do that when we're so far apart, in every possible way? The distance between us feels like an ocean, and I'm too scared to even try swimming across.

The urge to pour myself a drink is strong. I could just lose myself in a glass of whiskey, let it dull the edges of everything I'm feeling. But I know where that road leads, and I'm not going back there. I've fought too hard to stay on solid ground, and I'm not about to slip now.

Sitting here, alone in this quiet house, I can't help but feel the weight of it all. The loss of my family, the breakup with Lance—it's like a heavy blanket I can't shake off. It's why losing Lance hit me so hard; it wasn't just about him. It was about losing the future I thought I'd have. But even with everything that's happened, there's still this tiny spark of hope inside me, a dream of one day building a family of my own, of creating new memories to fill all these empty spaces.

THE NEXT MORNING, I SIT PATIENTLY IN FRONT OF WINTHROP Holdings headquarters. It's been nearly an hour since I followed her to this building, and I carefully watch the comings and goings of the morning. Fresh off the official release of the article to the public, I thought it imperative to compile as much evidence as I could to prove Quinn's guilt.

I hold a copy of the magazine I'd purchased earlier and study each word. I'm confident with this damning story and the ever-present correlations, I'd be able to secure a search warrant in no time. So now, I watch and wait, wait for her to make a mistake.

Suddenly, I see Quinn step outside, talking on her cellphone. She appears to be extremely frustrated. When she hangs up, I promptly hop out of my vehicle and approach her, holding the magazine.

"Mrs. Winthrop, good morning," I say.

"Detective," she replies. "Are you seriously still following me?"

"Me? Oh no, I'm just in the neighborhood. I stopped to pick up a magazine, actually," I say, holding it up.

"What do you want?" she asks, visibly vexed.

I mindlessly flip through the pages. "Have you seen this piece? I think it may interest you. It's an article about a supposed group of women who are murdering their husbands and getting away with it."

"Excuse me?" she says, her eyes narrowing.

"Here, you can have my copy. I picked up two. I have to say, this is movie-worthy stuff," I say with a chuckle, handing it to her.

She takes it, her expression a mix of confusion and ir-ritation.

I wink at her. "I'll be talking to you real soon," I call out as I get back into my car and drive off.

Back at the office, I go through the images I snapped the night before and send them in an email to Fatima.

Me:

Just sent you some images. Can you look through them when you get a chance? Let me know if any of those people are affiliated with that widow's ring.

Just as I hit send, Sergeant Sterling calls out from his of-fice, "Blaze!"

Nerves tingling with apprehension, I rise from my seat and walk to his office.

"Sir?" I say when I reach his door.

"Shut the door and sit down," he orders, his tone abrasive.

I do as I'm told, bracing myself for what is to come.

He stares at me, his eyes hard. "Guess who I just got a call from?"

"Sir?" I reply, trying to keep my voice steady.

"Quinn Winthrop's lawyer. Apparently, she feels that you've been harassing her. Which is peculiar because we closed the Winthrop case over a week ago. And I specifically told you to stand down," Sterling says with exasperation.

I quickly state, "I have reason to believe she was involved in her husband's death, sir. An article was released this morn-ing that is extremely damning. I know that she's involved. I can feel it."

Sterling's jaw tightens, his fingers drumming on the desk. "She's threatening to file a harassment claim against you, Blaze. This is serious. I told you to leave the Winthrop case alone."

"But sir," I plead, leaning forward, "the evidence in that article aligns perfectly with what we know. These women are part of a syndicate. They've been orchestrating the deaths of their wealthy husbands and making it look like accidents. We can't just ignore that."

Sterling's expression softens slightly, but his voice remains firm. "Blaze, I get that you're passionate about this. But we have procedures to follow. You can't just go rogue on us. There's a chain of command, and right now, you're stepping out of line."

"I understand that, sir. But if we don't act on this now, more people could die. We have to do something," I reason.

He sighs, rubbing his temples. "Look, Blaze, I know you're a good detective. One of the best. But you need to play this smart. We can't afford to have a harassment suit on our hands. You just got back, for goodness' sake. You need to back off for now. Let's see if we can find a way to approach this without stepping on any toes."

I nod reluctantly, knowing he's right but frustrated by the delay. "Copy that."

Sterling looks at me, a hint of concern in his eyes. "Be careful, Blaze. You've been through enough, and I don't want to see your career jeopardized over this."

"Thank you, sir," I say, standing up to leave. "I appreciate it."

"I hope to see you at Captain Wilson's retirement party," he says before I depart. It sounds much more like an order than a question.

I wasn't planning on it, but I quickly renege on my previous disposition. "Yes, sir, I'll be there."

As I walk out of his office, I can't shake the feeling of urgency. The truth is out there, and I'm determined to uncover it, no matter the cost. It infuriates me that I have to face such complications just to do my job. The fact is, Quinn has money, and money buys power, especially in high places. In contrast, deep down, I feel extremely frustrated and powerless, which I despise. My nerves start to get the best of me, so I grab my coat and head outside, desperate for some fresh air. Once outside, I breathe in the cool air and pace until I feel myself calm down.

"Are you okay?" a familiar voice says over my shoulder.

I turn and see Lance leaning against the wall, donning a suit topcoat and holding his briefcase. My stomach sinks. Great, interacting with him is the last fucking thing I need.

"What do you care?" I snort.

"Come on, Temp, don't be like that," he says, approaching me.

I challenge him, "How can you expect anything of me after all that has gone down, Lance?"

He sighs. "Look, I'm sorry."

I stare back at him, clearly struggling with navigating this new facet of our reality. The weight of knowing he's engaged now presses down on me, and I'm not sure if I want to bring it up. But the words slip out before I can stop them.

"I saw you with her, you know. Your fiancée." My voice is calm, but the tension in the air thickens instantly. Lance's expression falters just for a second, but it's enough to confirm that he wasn't expecting me to say anything about it.

"Temp..." he starts, but I cut him off.

"It's fine, Lance. Really. I hope you're happy," I say, trying to force a smile, though I'm not sure how convincing it is.

He nods, clearly uncomfortable, and the tension between us is apparent. For a moment, we're both silent, the weight of everything unsaid hanging between us.

I take a deep breath and let it out slowly, making peace with that thought. "Maybe we can be... friends," I say, my voice softening just a fraction.

He nods again, relief flickering in his eyes. "I'd like that, Temp. I really would."

THE NEXT MORNING, MY THOUGHTS ARE INTERRUPTED BY THE loud ring of my phone. Another case awaits, pulling me back into the unforgiving embrace of the city's underbelly. The rain beats against the windowpane, a somber backdrop to the grim scene awaiting me.

Twenty minutes later, I arrive at the crime scene, the rain continuing its relentless assault. My senses are immediately bombarded by the flurry of activity—medics, patrol officers, and the crime scene unit all working diligently to unravel the mystery before us. As I approach, I see the coroner's team retrieving the body from Wissahickon Creek. I make a mental note of every detail, my mind already racing with possibilities. Just then, Officer Marks, a friendly enough patrolman and steadfast presence amid the chaos, approaches.

"Detective Blaze, welcome back," Marks greets me, a hint of exhaustion in his voice.

"Thanks, Marks. How's fatherhood treating you?" I inquire, attempting to inject a note of warmth into the somber atmosphere.

He smiles wearily, pride evident in his tired eyes. "It's a blessing, Detective. Truly."

"That's good to hear," I reply, masking my own fatigue with a practiced smile.

When I approach to get a better glimpse at the deceased, the sight hits me like a sucker punch. I'm absolutely stunned to see Quinn Winthrop dead before me. With a newfound sense of urgency, I quickly assess her state, noticing cuts on her wrists. They're extremely deep and very precise, almost too precise.

CHAPTER
Fourteen

LOVER'S QUARREL

Halloween Night

Quinn stood in the dimly lit living room, her eyes fixed on the glass of cognac she'd just poured and placed onto the coffee table. A nagging realization gnawed at her—she had messed up. Her husband was still alive and breathing, which was not a part of the plan. She had been explicitly told to wait and be patient before going through this devious scheme, but she had ignored that advice, believing she could handle it her way.

Worse yet, she'd made the mistake of trusting Stormy to follow directions. Her associates had all done the deed themselves, insisting that it was the only way to ensure absolute success. But Quinn didn't want to risk getting her hands dirty, thinking she could control the situation from a distance. Now, that decision was coming back to haunt her. Her husband was painstakingly still alive.

Irritated, she pulled out a vial and stared at the poison that lay within her palm. The only logical explanation was that Stormy had failed to give Clay the drugs as instructed.

"It seems I have to do everything myself to ensure it's done correctly," she muttered, frustration boiling over as she carefully dropped the contents into the glass, watching the poison dissolve.

Clutching an envelope in her hand, she tightened her grip. Tonight, she would secure her freedom once and for all. Hearing keys rustle at the door, she squared her shoulders. Clay entered the rental property, shocked to see his wife. This was his escape from the tension of their cold home. Their eyes met, suspicion flickering in his.

"Quinn, what are you doing here?" he asked, his voice tense.

"Here, I believe you're going to need this," Quinn said, shoving the glass of cognac into Clay's hand with a tight-lipped smile. "We need to talk."

Clay, his brow furrowed in confusion, took the glass and hesitated before taking a sip. "Talk? About what? I thought you were supposed to be in New York."

Quinn's eyes narrowed as she followed him up the stairs, her voice dripping with contempt. "I want to talk about us, Clay. And I want to talk about your affair."

At the top of the stairs, Clay froze, his face draining of color. "What are you talking about?"

She watched with cold satisfaction as he took another sip of the cognac, oblivious to the poison swirling within it.

"Don't play dumb with me," she spat, pulling out the incriminating evidence and fanning it out in front of him like a deck of cards. "I have proof. Pictures of you and Stormy. You really think she would go for a piece of shit like you if I hadn't sent her your way?"

Clay's mouth hung open, his mind reeling as he processed her words. He downed the rest of the drink in one desperate gulp. "You paid Stormy to sleep with me?"

Quinn's lips twisted into a cruel smile, her tone ice-cold and unrelenting. "That's what she thinks. Getting her to sleep with you was merely an insurance policy if things didn't go my way. I paid her to kill you, but the stupid bitch didn't follow instructions."

She stepped closer, her eyes burning with years of pent-up rage. "You're a liar, a cheat, and a fucking disgrace, Clay. You've ruined everything you've touched, but I'm making sure you won't ruin me."

Clay's mind swirled with confusion. "Quinn, wait. Let's talk about this."

"Talk? You mean lie?" she retorted. "Here's the deal, honey. You're going to die tonight, and I'm going to get everything that I deserve."

"You can't be serious," he growled, anger twisting his face. "You've truly lost your fucking mind. Go home, Quinn."

"Call it whatever you want, Clay. Your time is up," she said with chilling assurance.

The anger radiated from his skin, and his chest heaved with fury. He lunged forward, trying to snatch the photos and choke her. In the struggle, his watch got caught on her bracelet and snapped off, clattering to the floor. They grappled at the top of the stairs, a tense, desperate fight for control.

"Clay, stop!" Quinn shouted, trying to push him away.

"You think you can threaten me and get away with it?" His voice was filled with accusation and fear.

Suddenly, the struggle halted. Both were breathing heavily, their eyes locked in a silent battle. Clay stepped back, his face twisted with confusion and anger.

"You are one crazy bitch," he muttered, turning his back on her to walk downstairs and pull out his phone.

Quinn's mind raced, wondering why the drugs were taking so long to work. Her heart pounded as she reached into her pocket to shove more down his throat if need be. But before she could act, Clay clutched his chest, pausing on the way down.

"Clay?" Quinn's voice wavered, a mix of shock and disbelief.

He stumbled, losing his balance. His hand reached out, grasping at the air, and then he fell. The sound of his body tumbling down the stairs was deafening, each thud echoing through the house. Quinn watched, frozen, as he came to a stop at the bottom, motionless.

For a moment, there was only silence. Quinn's breath caught in her throat as she slowly descended the stairs. She stopped a few steps away from his lifeless body, her eyes scanning his still form.

With a cold, detached calm, she nudged his outstretched hand with her stiletto, her mind already racing ahead to the next steps. As she turned to leave, a small, satisfied smile tugged at the corners of her mouth. The realization hit her—he was dead. A sense of relief washed over her, mingling with dark satisfaction.

CHAPTER
Fifteen

MASKS OFF

Stormy

Peering out at the city below, I'm stunned by certain realizations. Paige's gala was an eye-opening experience, to say the least. My instincts scream that Quinn had something to do with her husband's ultimate demise. Wrestling with this information all day has left me unsure of what to do about it. One thing is certain: the group Paige has found herself colluding with seems like a bunch of trouble I don't need.

Grabbing my tea, I sit on the couch, Zayn's words ringing in my head. How the hell did I manage to get sucked into all of this? Opening my laptop, I search for Gabrielle Dubois and am suddenly drawn into her opulent lifestyle filled with lavish events, elegance, and mystery. Once a model who migrated to the United States from Paris, Gabrielle married a rich man who died suddenly and has been a widow for the last twelve years. It seems to have served her well, achieving ultimate influence over the region's most prestigious circles.

There's something unsettling about her photo, something that feels eerily familiar. It's a look I recognize instantly—Gabrielle is a survivor, someone who has been through hell and back. Women like us, who've endured more than most can imagine, carry a certain aura, a steely resolve that only others who have walked the same dark path can see. She's the type who would go to any lengths to protect herself, to ensure she's never vulnerable again.

A sudden knock at my door startles me. I shut my laptop and get up to answer it. When I see Zayn, a sense of relief washes over me. He steps inside, looking distressed, and pulls me in for a hug. I take his hand, and we settle onto the couch. After our last encounter, I'm eager to hear an explanation.

The silence is uncomfortable.

"What are the chances that you're Paige's mysterious brother-in-law?" I say, trying to lighten the mood.

"Wild indeed," he replies with a half-smile. Zayn sighs, brushing his hand through his hair, obviously conflicted. "Dom and I share the same father, Nathaniel Hansen. He was a very wealthy man, and I only found out he was my father when he died and left me a large inheritance in his will."

I sit up, stunned by the connection. "I'm sure that was shocking."

He nods and continues, "Supposedly, he felt guilty for getting my mother pregnant and abandoning her to raise me on her own. Apparently, my father was sending her money to aid with my care under one condition: never tell anyone about him. My mother kept true to that promise until the day she died. I guess it was her assurance that I would be taken care of. After all, how do you tell your son that his white father doesn't want to acknowledge his Black son in public? It's pretty fucked up."

My heart aches for him. I know all too well the feeling of being rejected by your parents.

"At least I got a brother out of it. Dom spent the last few years going out of his way to get to know me. I didn't always make it easy. I was pretty pissed for a long time about everything. But slowly over time, I realized that none of this was Dom's fault. He was the only family I had left, and I wanted to work on our bond. We got close, all things considered. He even became a silent partner in my business." He pauses, clasping his hands together. "When he suddenly died, something seemed off. He had just taken a test to check his heart, and everything turned out good. Nothing was detected. I know this because he was urging me to do the same since our father died from heart failure."

"Zayn, what are you saying?" I ask.

His eyes lock with mine, searching for something. "Stormy, how much do you really know about Paige?"

"Enough," I say, my voice a bit too quick, a bit too sharp. "I've known her for a long time, I guess you could say. Zayn, what is it? What's going on?"

He hesitates for a moment as if weighing his words. "Her early life... it's muddy, to say the least. There are gaps and inconsistencies. I'm certain she's not who she claims to be."

A chill runs down my spine. I can feel my heart rate spike, guilt gnawing at me from the inside out.

Zayn catches the conflict in my eyes, the way my fingers fidget with the hem of my shirt. He steps closer, his expression softening. "Hey, it's okay," he murmurs, gently placing a hand on my arm. "You don't have to figure this out alone."

I nod, though the unease lingers, the weight of the secrets pressing down on me.

Zayn rises from the chair, rubbing his temples as he starts pacing back and forth. "There's no easy way to say this, but I don't think Dom's death was an accident."

"What?" My voice comes out sharper than I intended, the shock hitting me like a cold wave.

"I believe Paige had something to do with my brother's death. It's part of the reason I came back to Philly: to get the truth and justice he deserves," he says with certainty, which makes my skin hot.

The information is a whirlwind in my thoughts, and I struggle to find my words. Zayn walks back to the couch and sits down beside me, gently taking my hand in his. "Those women she's involved with, they're dangerous, Stormy. All their husbands have met a similar fate."

My chest tightens, making it hard to breathe.

"You have to promise to stay away from them," he pleads, looking deep into my eyes.

"I will," I say, my voice trembling.

THE MORNING LIGHT FILTERS THROUGH THE CURTAINS, GENTLY rousing me from sleep. As I slowly awaken, the events of the night before flood my mind. Zayn's revelation about his brother's death and his suspicions about Paige weigh heavily on me. Pushing the covers aside, I rise from the bed, pull a robe over my naked body, and make my way to the kitchen, where the aroma of breakfast greets me.

Zayn stands at the stove in boxers and nothing else, flipping pancakes with practiced ease. The sizzle of butter in the pan fills the air as I join him in the kitchen.

"Morning," he greets me with a warm smile, though there's a tension in his eyes that betrays his thoughts.

"Morning," I reply, taking a seat at the kitchen island. "Need any help?"

"Nah, I've got it covered," he says, turning off the stove and arranging the pancakes on a plate. "I've been making these since I was a kid."

As he sets the plate down in front of me, I can't help but feel grateful for his presence. Despite the turmoil surrounding us, his calm demeanor is a reassuring comfort.

"So, what's next?" I ask, taking a bite of my pancake. "Are you going to stay in Philly and see this through?"

Zayn pauses, considering my question. "Honestly, I'm not sure. My lawyer is urging me to let this all go. I've been thinking about leaving for a while now. This whole situation with Dom's death... it's made me realize that I need a fresh start."

A surprising pang of sadness tugs at my heart. I glance down, absentmindedly poking at my food. I've longed for a fresh start, too, but the thought of us finding new beginnings separately suddenly makes my palms sweat.

Zayn's expression softens, and he reaches across the table to take my hand. "I want you to come with me, Stormy."

I look into his eyes, stunned. Before I can respond, Zayn's phone buzzes on the counter. He picks it up, his brow furrowing as he reads the notification.

"What is it?" I ask, sensing the shift in his demeanor.

"It's an article," he says, his voice tense. "Something in *The Philadelphian Digest.*"

My heart skips a beat. "About what?"

Zayn's jaw tightens as he reads the feature, his expression growing grimmer with each passing second.

"It's all here," he says, his voice barely above a whisper. "And it might be enough to finally get justice for Dom."

Without another word, Zayn sets down his phone and rushes to grab his clothing. "I need to call my lawyer," he says, his voice urgent. "This changes everything."

Once dressed, he gives me a kiss and hurries out the door. I'm left alone in the kitchen, the weight of Zayn's words settling over me like a heavy blanket. The truth is finally starting to emerge from the shadows, and amid the chaos, a sense of fear grips me.

As the day wears on, I find myself caught up in the mundane tasks of cleaning my apartment. The sound of the vacuum fills the air, drowning out the chaos of my thoughts. I scrub furiously at the countertops, trying to distract myself from the whirlwind of emotions swirling inside me.

Zayn's revelation earlier still weighs heavily on my mind. I feel conflicted about the secrets I've been keeping. I know I should tell him about my involvement with Quinn and Clay, about my relationship with Paige—hell, my real name, even. But the words stick in my throat, trapped by fear and uncertainty.

Just as I'm lost in my thoughts, my phone rings, jolting me back to reality. I glance at the caller ID and see Paige's name flashing on the screen. My stomach sinks, and I contemplate whether I should answer or not. As I do, Zayn's warning plays over and over again in my mind. If Paige is as dangerous as he thinks she is, it's probably best not to tip her off. With a sigh, I answer the call, readying myself for whatever she has to say.

"Hello?" I say, trying to keep my voice steady.

"Well, you made quite an impression on Gabrielle," Paige says.

My heart skips a beat at the mention of Gabrielle's name.

Paige continues, "She asked me to invite you over for dinner."

"That's... unexpected," I say, struggling to mask my surprise. "Why me?"

She sighs. "I don't know. Maybe she just wants to get to know you better."

"Although I'm flattered, I'm not sure I can make it," I say.

"I hope you're still not mad about the other night," she says with a snort.

I stay silent, the tension thick in the air.

Her tone shifts subtly. "Listen, Storm, you don't decline invitations from Gabrielle Dubois," Paige asserts, her voice tinged with envy. "Do you realize how long it took for her to even acknowledge my existence? And now, here you are, she's specifically requesting your presence."

I hold my breath, half-expecting an apology that never comes. Finally, I let out a deep sigh and say, "Yeah, maybe. Can I get back to you?" My mind races with possibilities.

"Sure, but don't make me wait too long," she says. Suddenly, Paige inquires, her voice casual but probing. "So, how do you know Zayn? I saw you two talking before you left without saying goodbye."

I freeze, my heart pounding in my chest. "Oh, we just... bumped into each other at Ashton's," I lie, the words tasting bitter on my tongue. "I don't know him like that."

Her silence speaks volumes, and I can practically feel her suspicion radiating through the phone.

Changing the subject, I ask, "How do you know Quinn? I was surprised to see her at your party as well."

Paige's tone carries a weight of solemnity as she speaks, "I do... well, I did."

Perplexed, I inquire, "What do you mean?"

Her tone shifts, filled with a mix of surprise and disbelief, "You haven't heard?"

I shake my head, feeling a growing sense of dread, "Heard what?"

In a somber tone, Paige reveals, "Girl, they found her floating in the river yesterday. Apparently, the recent death of her husband was too much, and she took her own life."

My heart sinks, the news hitting me like a ton of bricks. "What?"

Paige's words hit me like a sudden downpour, casting a dark cloud over our conversation. "I know it's wild. But hey, you got paid, right?"

Confusion creeps into my voice as I raise an eyebrow. "What are you talking about?"

There's a hint of smugness in her tone as she replies, "You know, the arrangement. Quinn paid up, didn't she?"

My heart sinks as her admission settles in. She's confessing to orchestrating it all. "Wait, you set this whole thing up?"

She dismisses my surprise with a casual flick of her teeth. "Come on, Storm. You got your cut. What's the big deal?"

"The big deal?" I snap back, my frustration boiling over. "They're both dead!"

Paige's tone remains eerily composed. "This was going to play out regardless. That's the game, right? You know this. Besides, you didn't kill them. You're in the clear. You got what you wanted. You're welcome."

My breath catches in my throat as I reel from her callousness. Zayn's warning echoes loudly in my mind. This woman is not to be trusted.

"What do you mean by 'killed'?" I press, seeking clarity.

She brushes off my question. "You're really tripping."

"I can't do this," I mutter, ending the call abruptly. Nausea churns in my stomach as I stumble to the bathroom, the weight of her words heavy on my conscience.

That night, while I settle into the soft cushions of my couch, the sultry tone of Carmen Jones wraps around me like a familiar embrace, providing a much-needed escape from the swirling chaos of my life. A smile graces my lips as I indulge in the timeless allure of the film. Dorthy Dandridge's portrayal of Carmen captivates me once again, just as it did when I watched it with my mom as a child.

I'm mesmerized by the power, fearlessness, and allure of this Black woman on the screen. Each scene resonates deeply, reminding me of the strength and resilience within myself. Sipping a glass of red wine, its warmth soothes me, momentarily easing the tension in my body. As night descends, casting long shadows across the walls of my apartment, I find a brief solace from the revelations of the day. Just then, my phone softly chimes.

Zee:

> Your items are ready.

I stare at the words, lost in thought, contemplating my next move. I could leave right now, start over, and leave this dark storm and all my ties to it behind. Maybe I should go to Tempest—she's a cop, after all. She could help me untangle this mess. But how much would I have to reveal? Temp doesn't know about my life choices, and I'm not sure I'm ready for her to. The idea of leaving with Zayn keeps tugging at me, offering a clean break and a fresh start far from here. But how can I do that knowing I'm still lying to him? The weight of indecision is suffocating as I struggle to find the right path in the midst of all this chaos.

Suddenly, a sharp knock shatters the silence of the night, jolting me from my thoughts. I pause the movie and set my glass aside, my heart racing with anticipation as I approach the door. With trembling hands, I reach for the handle and swing it open.

And there, standing before me, is a figure from my past. Shock courses through me, leaving me momentarily speechless as I lock eyes with my sister, Tempest.

CHAPTER
Sixteen

SISTERS IN THE SHADOWS

Tempest

s I stand in the doorway of Jada's place, the contrast between now and our last meeting almost a year ago is stark. Her gaze meets mine, unreadable, leaving me uncertain of her reception. Will she welcome me with open arms or shut me out completely again? Surprisingly, she steps aside, wordlessly inviting me in.

Our hug is awkward, tension crackling between us like static electricity. "This is a surprise," Jada says once we part, her voice tinged with a mixture of curiosity and caution.

I scratch my temple, realizing I haven't fully thought through this impromptu visit. "Yeah, sorry to pop up on you like this," I mumble, my words feeling inadequate.

Quinn's death set off alarm bells in my mind, pushing me to thoroughly search the Winthrop residence, trusting my gut that things weren't as they seemed. The suicide story? I didn't buy it—not for a second. It all felt too convenient, too staged, especially considering the substantial financial settlement Quinn was about to receive. I couldn't believe she'd suddenly be overcome with guilt over killing her husband, a theory I still hold. As I combed through her belongings, hoping to piece together the final hours of her life, my instincts kept screaming that something was off.

Then I found them—a thumb drive and manila folder tucked away, almost as if it was begging to be found. On it were photos and video of Clay Winthrop and Jada, caught in compromising positions that left little to the imagination. The shock of seeing my sister in the middle of this mess hit me like a ton of bricks. My immediate reaction was to keep this discovery to myself. But the conflict inside me was growing—what has she gotten herself into, and how can I help her without revealing everything I've found?

The weight of this new information presses down on me, and I know I can't leave this alone. I need answers, and more importantly, I need to protect Jada before this whole situation spirals even further out of control. I can't shake the feeling that she's not entirely pleased to see me after all this time, and I wonder if she suspects the real reason for my visit.

"Would you like some tea?" she asks, cutting through the tension in the air.

"Yes, thank you."

As she disappears into the kitchen, I take a moment to absorb my surroundings. Memories flood back, reminding me of the bond we once shared. But time has changed us, and I wonder if we'll ever reclaim what we've lost.

Walking through her home, I'm struck by its magnificence, a reflection of her extravagant taste. The high ceilings, adorned with floor-to-ceiling windows, offer a breathtaking view of the city skyline. Chic yet simple decor fills the space, a testament to her elegance. It's a far cry from the humble surroundings we once shared as young girls.

When Jada returns, we settle into the living room with our tea. "Your place is phenomenal. It's really come along," I comment, genuinely impressed by the transformation.

"Thanks," she replies softly, her eyes flickering with a mix of pride and something else—perhaps fear. The silence stretches between us, filled with unspoken questions and the weight of our shared history.

I take a sip of my tea, trying to gather my thoughts. "Jada," I begin cautiously, "I need to talk to you about something important. It's about a case that I'm working on."

Her expression shifts, concern etched on her face. "Okay, what's that have to do with me?" she inquires, her tone softening.

My voice holds steady. "How well do you know the Winthrops?"

I can sense my question has thrown her completely off guard. "I don't know what you mean."

With a deep breath, I dig into my bag and retrieve a manila file folder. Passing it to her, I elaborate. "I found something," I say, choosing my words carefully. "They're of you and Mr. Winthrop. I also found your telephone number on both of their phones. I need to understand what your connection is to all of this."

Jada's eyes widen, and she looks away, her hands clenched tightly in her lap. The silence between us feels heavier, filled with the weight of her secrets.

"The other night, you were at a gala event, the same gala Quinn attended," I continue, my voice trembling slightly. "Are you affiliated with those women in any way?"

The tension in the room intensifies as she denies any involvement, though her eyes betray a flicker of doubt.

"Let me help you, Jada," I plead, desperation creeping into my voice. "Do you have any information? Anything at all?"

"What? No," she says quickly.

Jada walks to the window, gazing out at the night sky as if searching for answers. "All I know is that their marriage was far from perfect, obviously," she replies, her voice tinged with sadness.

"Do you know why or how she got this evidence of you with her husband?" I press, my heart pounding in my chest.

She turns to face me, her expression a mix of confusion and frustration. "Don't do that. Don't you dare judge me, Tempest," she snaps.

Quickly, I shake my head, denying any judgment. "No, Jada, of course I'm not," I assure her, my voice filled with sincerity.

But her anger flares, her words laced with bitterness. "How dare you? I'm sorry we can't excel at college and make something of ourselves, Tempest. Everything I've done up to this point is to survive."

Feeling a sting of guilt, I reach out to reassure her. "Jada, I didn't mean to offend you. I'm just trying to get to the bottom of this," I protest, my voice tinged with regret.

My eyes trail behind her as she strides through her place toward the door. With a swift motion, she unlocks it and swings it open, then turns to face me.

"Well, it looks like you've got a lot of work to do. Please leave," Jada says, her tone firm.

I stand up, feeling a rush of emotions but unable to find the right words to express them. Hurt and rejected, I gather my things, swallowing back tears as I prepare to leave. "I'm sorry for everything, Jada. I know you don't believe me, but I am," I murmur, my voice trembling with emotion.

As I stand on the threshold, staring into her cold, unwelcoming eyes, a twinge of longing for the sisterhood we once shared cuts through me. But her silence says it all, deepening the divide between us. She closes the door, leaving me alone with nothing but my regrets.

CHAPTER
Seventeen

SILENT NIGHT, SHATTERED BONDS

Tempest

Two years earlier…

As Lance and I approach Jada's door, a deep sense of uncertainty grips me, tightening like an unwelcome embrace around my chest. It's Christmas, and I'm trying my best to put on a good face for my sister, but the weight of the past week feels crushing, the doctor's devastating words echoing in my mind like a haunting melody. Lance's concern is clear, his eyes searching mine for reassurance before he knocks on the door, but it's not something that I can fully give.

The memory of the miscarriage is vivid—the blood, the searing pain, and the hot tears that seemed endless. I remember the overwhelming sense of failure, the embarrassment of not being able to carry life within me, the dream of motherhood slipping through my fingers like sand. The shame of *feeling inadequate, of being unable to fulfill what I believed was my most basic role, gnaws at me constantly.*

And then there's the agonizing suspicion that the stress from my job played a role in all of this. The late nights, the constant pressure, the weight of the cases that never leave my mind—it all feels like it might have contributed to this loss.

Lance's gentle kiss on my hand offers a fleeting moment of comfort, but it's not enough to erase the deep scars left behind. As much as I try to gather the pieces of myself, the wound is still fresh, and I can't help but wonder if it will ever truly heal.

People say these things happen as if that's supposed to make it easier to bear. But for me, it only deepens the emptiness, leaving me adrift in a sea of grief.

Seconds later, the door swings open, revealing Jada's birth mother, Mabel—a surprising sight given her history of unreliability. She looks different, better even, but skepticism claws at my gut. An older, weathered version of her daughter, Mabel bears the marks of a hard life, and I can't help but question the sincerity of her apparent transformation.

"Tempest, honey, it's so good to see you," Mabel greets me with a kiss on the cheek, her warmth unfamiliar against my skin.

"Hi, Mabel," I respond, my tone guarded.

Mabel's attention turns to Lance, her smile brightening. "And who might this handsome man be?"

"Lance, my boyfriend," I introduce, tension tainting my words.

"It's nice to meet you," Lance says, offering a polite smile.

The exchange of pleasantries does little to ease my unease as Mabel leads us inside, her cheerful demeanor grating on my nerves.

"We brought some apple pie and wine," Lance says, gesturing toward the items in his hands.

"That's so sweet of you, let me take that," Mabel replies graciously, accepting the offerings.

As Mabel disappears into the kitchen with the pie and wine, a sense of suspicion settles over me. Despite her apparent sobriety, something feels off—I just can't bring myself to trust her. But for Jada's sake, I push aside my doubts and follow Lance into the warmth of her home.

"Where's Jada?" I inquire, scanning the room for my sister.

"She'll be out in a minute," Mabel replies, excitement evident in her voice.

Just then, Jada emerges from her bedroom, her face radiant with joy. "Merry Christmas, family!"

We share a warm hug, momentarily dispelling the tension in the air.

"Hey, Lance! Happy holidays, bro," Jada greets Lance with a hearty embrace.

Over dinner, we indulge in a feast of holiday classics—pot roast, stuffing, candied yams, and collard greens. The dishes, passed down from Mabel's mother, carry with them a sense of tradition and nostalgia.

I had hoped to find a moment alone with Jada, a chance to confide in her about the miscarriage and the turmoil I've been struggling with. But it's as though Mabel is purposely hogging all of Jada's attention, constantly chattering, leaving no room for a private conversation. It irritates me more than I care to admit, and I can't shake the growing resentment toward Jada's easy forgiveness of Mabel's past transgressions.

Their laughter fills the room, a stark reminder of their bond. Each shared joke stings with jealousy, a bitter reminder of my own pain. Despite Lance's concerned gaze, I drown my sorrows in wine, seeking solace in its numbing embrace.

As I raise my glass to my lips, Lance's voice cuts through the chatter. "Maybe you should take it easy," he whispers in my ear.

Ignoring his warning, I fixate on Jada and Mabel across the table, frustration bubbling to the surface. "I'm fine," I insist, my voice strained.

Their laughter grates on my nerves, each giggle a jab at the wounds I'm trying to hide. I can no longer contain my resentment.

With a bitter sip of wine, I interrupt their banter, "What's so fuck-ing funny?"

Jada

I STARE AT TEMPEST, STUNNED BY HER SUDDEN OUTBURST. CAN'T SHE see how much this moment means to me? Sitting at this dinner table, surrounded by the people I love most, is a rare blessing. I was genuinely excited about the holiday festivities, even if Ms. Gwen and Mr. Lewis couldn't join us because she fell unexpectedly ill. It would have been perfect with them here, but I'm determined to make the most of this night either way.

Tempest's skepticism toward my mother, Mabel, isn't unfounded. She's been by my side supporting me when my mother let me down so many times before, but I'd much rather keep that in the past. People deserve forgiveness, don't they? Despite her flaws, she's still my mother, my family.

No, Tempest and I are not blood, but she is my family, too. I just want all of us to get along and grow together. I glance at Tempest, understanding the weight she carries—the tragic loss of her parents, the years spent in foster care with no one to call family, how much she struggled with her guilt, and finding ways to make the most of her life. I know work has been stressful for her lately. Because of this, I can't help but feel a sense of sadness for her, knowing she would give anything to have a moment like this with her own mother and father.

"I hope you all saved room for dessert," I announce, determined to salvage the evening.

Without objection, I rise from my seat and hurry to the kitchen, eager to distract myself from the task at hand. As I gather dessert plates and cutlery, my thoughts drift to the lemon pound cake I made earlier with the *help of my mother. Today was supposed to be special, and I refuse to let anything or anyone spoil it.*

In the kitchen, I overhear snippets of conversation between my mother and Tempest. Concern creeps into my heart as I listen, hoping everything is okay.

"Tempest, are you all right, honey? You seem upset," Mabel's voice is filled with genuine concern.

Tempest's response is cold, "I'm fine. Please don't come in here pretending to care about anyone but yourself."

I hesitate for a moment, debating whether to intervene. My mother urges gently, "Take it easy, honey."

But Tempest's tone grows sharper, her words slicing through the air like a blade. "Don't tell me to take it easy. You can run that tired game on Jada but not on me. I see you for exactly who you are—selfish. You toy with your daughter, getting her hopes up, stringing her along just to let her down, time and time again. What's your game, Mabel? Money? How much do you need this time?"

My mother's voice trembles. "I-I don't know what you're talking about."

"You know exactly what I'm talking about, and I'm sick of it! You never deserved to be a mother. All you care about is being a pathetic, waste-of-life junkie!" she screams.

The accusation hangs heavy in the air, and a knot forms in my stomach. I rush back into the dining room, my heart pounding.

My mother's expression crumples with hurt, stopping me in my tracks. The pain in her eyes is unmistakable.

"I, um, I think that I should go," she manages to say.

With a heavy heart, my mother excuses herself and leaves, and I'm left standing in the dining room, feeling the weight of the evening's events pressing down on me. The warmth I felt just moments ago is replaced by a cold emptiness.

"Why did you have to do that?" I shout, my voice trembling with anger and hurt.

Tempest, standing across from me, eyes blazing with a mixture of guilt and defiance, snaps back, "You know why, Jada! You just refuse to see it. She's using you!"

"You think I don't know that?" I scoff, my voice dripping with sarcasm. "Sorry if I want to enjoy my mother while she is still here. You, of all people, know we only get one mother, Tempest."

"Oh really? How many chances in life is your mother going to get?" she retorts, her words laced with venom. "Sometimes I think you'd be better off if she was dead."

The words hit me like a punch to the gut, knocking the wind out of me. I stand there, stunned, the room spinning as her words sink in. The depth of her anger, her bitterness, feels like a betrayal, cutting through whatever bond we once shared. My chest tightens with a mix of rage and sorrow, my hands trembling at my sides as I try to process what she just said.

The silence between us is thick, suffocating as we stand there, staring each other down. The realization that our relationship might be damaged beyond repair looms over us, a truth I can't ignore.

CHAPTER
Eighteen

MATTERS OF THE HEART

Tempest

That evening, I stare at myself in the rearview mirror, taking a few deep breaths to calm my nerves. My body is tense, still frazzled from my encounter with Jada. Memories of that fateful Christmas night haunt me. I regret everything and wish I could take it back. But I can't—the damage is done. Jada could barely even look at me, and now I understand just how deeply our rift has affected her and me.

Our relationship wasn't just damaged that night—it was shattered. I tried countless times to reach out, to apologize, and to make things right, but each attempt was met with cold silence. The confrontation that night did more than just drive a wedge between us; it sent Mabel back into the depths of addiction—a relapse that Jada would never forgive me for. The weight of that knowledge crushes me, knowing that my words, my actions, might have pushed Mabel over the edge for good this time. The realization that I may have lost my sister, not just physically but emotionally, cuts deeper than any pain I've ever known. Now, I'm left with nothing but the haunting memories of what once was and the bitter reality of what could never be repaired.

I take another deep breath before walking into Mikey's Pub. Inside, my colleagues are full of life, laughing and celebrating our captain's much-deserved retirement after thirty years of service. The ceiling is decorated with streamers and balloons, and there's a setup for cake and gifts, along with an array of pictures detailing Captain Wilson's decorated career.

I quickly find a seat at the bar and order a club soda, trying to stay grounded as the party buzzes around me. Moments later, Maldonado walks in, hand in hand with a beautiful Asian woman. When they spot me, they make their way over, and I force a smile, determined not to let the weight of the day drag me down.

"Blaze! This is my friend Cassie," Maldonado says, her voice light.

Cassie extends her hand. "Nice to meet you."

We shake hands, and they take the seats beside me, chatting about lighter things. McGregor is in rare form tonight, rallying the crowd with his usual enthusiasm. "Shots! Get us shots!" he hollers to the bartender.

I watch as the bartenders line up over thirty shots, distributing them across the bar. When McGregor hands one to me, I hesitate, the familiar weight of the glass suddenly feeling heavier. It's been over ten months since I last had a drink, not since that night—the night everything spiraled out of control after Lance left me. That night ended with an overdose and a painful truth I'd been avoiding for too long: I was an addict.

I turned to alcohol and pills to cope with the miscarriage and the fallout with Jada, using it as a crutch to numb the pressures, pain, and chaos that was my life. It took me a while to come to grips with the reality of my addiction. Now, I'm just trying to navigate life sober, trying to grow from the wreckage of my past. But tonight, with all the shit I've been dealing with, the temptation is stronger than ever. Maybe just one drink wouldn't hurt.

As I wrestle with the urge, a sting of guilt hits me when I think about that night with Mabel. I was so hard on her, so judgmental. But now, I get it. I understand the struggles of addiction in a way I never could before. The need to escape, to drown out the pain, is something I've fought myself. The realization leaves me feeling conflicted, caught between my own struggles and the understanding that addiction isn't something you just snap out of—it's a battle, one I now know all too well.

Before I can fully think it through, I toss back the shot. The burn of the alcohol ignites a familiar fire in my veins, a rush of energy that feels dangerously good. I close my eyes, relishing the sensation. Maybe this is exactly what I needed, a small escape from the mess that my life has always been.

A few minutes later, the energy ramps up, and the bar is filled with laughter and conversation. I'm feeling much more relaxed and at ease. When I see Lance walking in, my heart drops.

Before I can stop myself, I turn to the bartender. "Hey, give me another shot, please."

I watch as she pours me another, the amber liquid glistening under the bar lights. I take a deep breath, trying to push down the nagging voice in the back of my mind, and quickly toss it back. The warmth spreads through me, a temporary relief from everything weighing me down.

"Tempest, how are you?" Lance's voice breaks through my thoughts as he approaches, his expression instantly concerned.

I turn to him, surprised to see him here. "Honestly, I could be better. You?"

He studies me for a moment before responding. "I didn't think I'd see you here tonight. You know, after everything. Is everything okay? Are you still adjusting to work?"

"I guess you could say that." I sigh, the weight of everything heavy on my shoulders.

"Give yourself some time," he says, his tone gentle. "You're a great detective, Temp. And you've been through a lot."

I give him a small smile, appreciating his words even if they feel distant. "Truthfully, it's that, and knowing I'd run into you sooner or later. I don't know how to be around you just yet, after everything, you know?"

He nods, and for a brief moment, there's a flicker of something in his eyes—remorse, maybe. "I get it. I feel the same. I struggled quite a bit when things ended, too."

His confession catches me off guard. "You did?"

Lance's gaze softens, and he offers a small nod. "Yeah, I did. It wasn't easy, Temp. But I want you to know I'm here if you need someone to talk to."

His words hang in the air, a mix of sincerity and an attempt to be cordial. It's strange, this new dynamic between us, and I'm not sure how to navigate it just yet.

Deep down, I wasn't sure he even cared. A part of me always suspected he judged me for how I handled things that night at Jada's. Another part of me often wondered if he secretly blamed me for the miscarriage or if he stayed with me afterward out of pity rather than love. Whatever the reason, when he left, it felt like he took a big piece of my heart with him.

As if reading my mind, Lance says quietly, "Temp, I loved you immensely. I just couldn't help you."

I swallow hard, trying to keep my emotions in check. "Then how could you move on so fast? You're engaged, Lance."

His eyes flicker with something—guilt, maybe regret. "It wasn't easy, Temp. I tried to cope in my own way, just like you did. But... things happened, and I met someone who helped me move forward. It doesn't mean I've forgotten or that I never cared."

I nod, but the ache in my chest only deepens. "I just... it feels like you left me in the dust, Lance. Like everything we went through didn't matter."

"It mattered," he says softly. "It mattered more than you know."

Just then, McGregor approaches with more shots. Lance shakes his head, declining, and leaves us to our conversation.

"I'm sorry for putting all of that on you. It wasn't fair," I say, my voice wavering slightly.

Lance looks at me, his expression softening. "I appreciate that," he replies.

My eyes start to gloss over with unshed tears. "Are you happy?" I ask, almost afraid to hear the answer.

He hesitates for a moment before nodding. "Yes, I am."

"What's her name?" I ask, even though the words feel like they're ripping me apart.

"Her name is Naya," he says, a small smile tugging at the corners of his lips. "She's a professor—smart, kind, really great with people."

I force a smile, but inside, my heart is breaking all over again. "She sounds amazing," I manage to say, though every word feels like it's pulling me deeper into the abyss.

"She is," Lance agrees, and the warmth in his voice is almost unbearable to hear.

My throat tightens, but I push it all down, trying to maintain some semblance of composure. "I'm glad you found someone who makes you happy," I say, though it takes everything in me to get the words out.

"Thanks, Temp," he says softly, his gaze lingering on mine as if he knows how hard this is for me. "I really hope you find that too, someday."

I nod, unable to trust my voice to respond. As much as I want to be happy for him, the pain of knowing he's truly moved on is almost too much to bear.

"Are you all right?" Lance asks, concern evident in his eyes.

I nod weakly. "Yeah, well, no. I just had a drink—two, actually—after almost a year of being sober. God, I'm truly a mess."

The truth is, the alcohol is starting to hit me just as another round of shots is being passed around. I try to shake off the dizziness and pick up another shot. "Hey, third time's a charm, right?" I say, forcing a smile before tossing it back with the others.

Lance's eyes narrow with worry as he watches me. "Temp, don't throw away all you've worked for, it's not worth it. Let me get you home," he says, his voice gentle but firm, clearly concerned about where this might lead.

"I'm okay," I slur.

"No, you're not. Give me your keys," his voice is assertive.

He helps me into my car, and I can't help but notice the familiar scent of his cologne, more intoxicating than the alcohol. My mind is swirling with so many thoughts and feelings—being this close to him again is overwhelming, stirring up memories I thought I'd buried. I close my eyes, trying to escape the whirlwind inside me, and soon drift off to sleep.

Fifteen minutes later, I feel Lance's gentle tap on my knee. I struggle to open my eyes, feeling groggy and disoriented, but I manage to get out of the car with his help. He guides me up the steps and onto the porch, his touch steady and familiar. When he uses my keys to unlock the door, I can't help but feel a sting of heartache. Seeing him like this, back in the place we once called home, is almost too much to bear. The way we used to be—sharing this space, in love, with our future so bright—feels like a distant dream now, one that's slipping further away with each passing moment.

"I miss you so much, Lance," I blurt out before I can stop myself.

He turns back to look at me, a smile slightly covering his lips. Lance helps me into the house, through the entryway, then the living room, settling me onto the couch. I watch, unsure if he'd heard me, petrified that he's ignoring me.

He kneels to untie and slip off my boots, his fingers grazing my skin, sending shivers up my spine. Once done, he sighs and stares into the deepest depths of my soul. "I miss you too," he murmurs, his voice thick with longing. He leans in, kissing me deeply, his passion and fire igniting something within me.

In my bedroom, the air is thick with anticipation as our lips meet again, this time with a fervor that speaks to the time we've spent apart. The familiar rhythm of our bodies syncs effortlessly as if no time has passed at all. His hands roam over me, rekindling the fire that once burned so brightly between us.

He reaches over to the nightstand, his movements confident and sure, retrieving a condom from the drawer. The shiny gold wrapper catches the dim light as he tears it open with his teeth, his eyes never leaving mine. The sight of his pearly whites against his dark skin as he prepares to make love to me sends a thrill down my spine.

Our eyes lock as he slides the condom on, and I can feel the heat radiating between us, intensifying with every second. He leans in for another kiss, and as our lips meet, he enters me with a deep, deliberate thrust. The sensation sends a jolt of pleasure through me, and I gasp, wrapping my legs around his waist and pulling him even closer. My arms encircle his shoulders, holding on as he drives deeper and deeper, filling every part of me with his presence.

He shifts us, rolling me onto my side, entering me from behind with a sensual ease. His fingers trace a fiery path along my outer thigh, each touch igniting a fresh wave of desire. My skin tingles under his caress, and I close my eyes, losing myself in the blissful sensations that are almost too intense to bear.

His arms wrap around me, pulling me closer, his breath hot against my neck as he whispers my name, "Tempest."

I arch my back, pressing myself against him, our bodies moving together in perfect harmony. My moans fill the room, mingling with the sound of our synchronized breathing as the dark shadows of our figures dance on the wall, a testament to the passion between us.

His pace quickens, driving me closer to the edge with every thrust, the tension within me building to an almost unbearable peak. With one final, powerful movement, I shatter, my body convulsing in a wave of pure ecstasy. He follows soon after, our bodies slick with sweat and the satisfaction of our reunion.

We collapse together, still wrapped in each other's arms, the aftermath of our lovemaking leaving us breathless and content. The room is silent now, save for the sound of our heavy breathing, and as I lay there in his embrace, everything in the world feels right, even if just for this moment.

A FEW HOURS LATER, I STIR AWAKE. I ROLL OVER, REACHING FOR Lance, wanting him again. But to my surprise, he's not there. Instead, he's seated at the foot of the bed, tying his shoes. The sight of him there, half-dressed and distant, sends a chill through me.

Sitting up, the sheets wrapped around my naked body, I whisper, "Stay."

He looks back at me, his eyes filled with a mix of sorrow and regret. "I can't," he says softly.

"Why not?" I ask, my voice trembling, though deep down, I know the answer.

Lance sighs, his shoulders slumping as he avoids my gaze. "Tempest, this... tonight... it was a mistake. We can't go back to how things were. I'm engaged now. I shouldn't have done this."

His words pierce through me like a dagger, the reality of the situation settling in. Tears welling up in my eyes, I plead, "Can't we at least try?"

He stands up, buttoning his shirt with a heavy heart. "It's not that simple. We both know that. There's too much pain, too much history. I don't want to hurt you more than I already have."

"You're hurting me now," I say, my voice breaking. "Leaving like this, it's breaking my heart all over again."

Lance walks over to me, brushing a tear from my cheek. "I'm sorry, Temp. I really am. But staying will only make things worse. You deserve someone who can give you everything, and right now, I'm not that person. What happened tonight—it was a moment of weakness, maybe even a need for closure on my part, but it can't go further than this."

I grab his hand, trying to hold onto the last bit of hope. "We can work through it, Lance. We can figure it out together."

He gently pulls his hand away, his expression pained. "I wish we could. But some things are just too broken to fix."

With that, he turns and walks out of the bedroom, leaving me sitting there, feeling more alone than ever. The sound of the front door opening and then closing echoes through the empty house, a stark reminder of the finality of his departure.

I collapse back onto the bed, clutching the sheets to my chest, sobs racking my body. The weight of his absence presses down on me, and I can't escape the crushing realization that he's gone—again. In the quiet darkness, I'm left alone with my thoughts, the unbearable ache of a broken heart, and the knowledge that this time, it's truly over.

CHAPTER

Nineteen

DARK SHADOWS

Stormy

It's been twenty-four hours since Tempest's unexpected visit, and anxiety grips my chest like a tight knot. Her questions about my involvement with the Winthrops replay in my mind, and I can't shake the dread that hangs over me. I know I should talk to someone, but trusting Tempest is still a struggle. Surprisingly enough, I feel like I can trust Zayn. There's something about him, something steady and reassuring, which makes me believe he won't judge me.

With trembling fingers, I send him a text, hoping that opening up to him will finally give me the relief I desperately need.

Me:

I need to speak to you. It's urgent.

Feeling too restless to stay cooped up, I decide to get dressed and go for a walk to clear my head. The crisp night air feels like a soothing on my frazzled nerves. My high heels carry me through the city until I find myself at the Rodin Museum. The peaceful atmosphere and beautiful sculptures seem to offer a temporary refuge from my racing thoughts.

As I wander through the historical museum, the serene beauty of the sculptures covers me in a sense of tranquility. Each masterpiece seems to hold a story of its own, offering a glimpse into the human experience and the complexities of emotion.

I stop before "The Thinker," its imposing figure casting a shadow over the garden. The sculpture's contemplative pose resonates with me, mirroring the tumultuous thoughts swirling in my mind. I wonder what secrets lie behind the stoic façade, what inner conflict they grapple with.

As I explore further, I find myself drawn to "The Kiss," a masterpiece of passion and desire. The lovers' embrace speaks of an intensity that transcends time and space, igniting a longing within me for connection and understanding.

Suddenly, a voice speaks from over my shoulder, sending shock waves through my body. "Stormy! Bonjour, what a pleasant surprise," Gabrielle Dubois says, her voice coated with warmth.

When I turn around to face her, I see her eyes light up with recognition and something more—an insistence I can't quite place. There's something that I can't quite ignore with this woman. And given the connections with Paige, Quinn, and all the death that seems to follow, I don't want to know.

"Gabrielle, it's great to see you," I reply, opting to play it cool.

She takes my hand, and her shadow of an associate watches our exchange, always within arm's reach. "Did Paige tell you about the dinner party that I am hosting tomorrow evening?"

I nod. "Yes, she did. I'm not sure I'll be able to make it, unfortunately."

"You must join us, darling. I won't take no for an answer," she urges with a sugarcoated smile and uncomfortable persistence.

Before I can utter a reply, my phone rings. It's Zayn.

"I have to take this, please excuse me. It was great seeing you," I say quickly, stepping away, eager to put some distance between us.

Outside, I eagerly answer my phone, "Hello?"

Relief floods through me when I hear his voice. "Is everything all right? Where are you?" he asks, his voice steady and reassuring.

"I took a walk to clear my head. I'm at the Rodin Museum," I reply, looking around.

"Stay there. I'm on my way," he says, and the call ends abruptly.

Moments later, I see Zayn pull up in front of the museum on a sleek motorcycle. He looks every bit the knight in shining armor, and I can't help but feel a flutter of excitement mixed with relief.

"Get on," he says, holding out a helmet for me.

I don't hesitate. I climb onto the motorcycle behind him, wrapping my arms tightly around his waist. The engine roars, and we speed off into the night.

The crisp fall air whips past us as we cruise down Benjamin Franklin Parkway. The trees lining the street are ablaze with autumn colors, their leaves rustling in the wind. The city lights blur into a dazzling array of colors, casting a surreal glow on everything around us. It's a perfect blend of exhilaration and peace, the kind I've been craving.

As we ride, I rest my head against Zayn's back, letting the steady rhythm of the motorcycle's engine soothe my anxious thoughts. For a moment, I forget about the secrets, the lies, and the weight of the world pressing down on my shoulders. All that matters is the open road ahead and the warmth of Zayn's presence.

We continue down the parkway, the beauty of the cityscape unfolding before us. The majestic Art Museum looms in the distance, its lights shimmering like a beacon. It's a perfect night, and for a brief time, everything feels right.

As Zayn's motorcycle purrs along Kelly Drive, the wind whips through my hair, carrying away some of the weight that's been burdening me. We find a quiet spot along the path, where the moon casts a soft glow on the water, and we sit in silence for a moment, taking in the peacefulness of the night.

I take a deep breath, gathering the courage to tell Zayn the truth. "Zayn, there's something I need to tell you," I begin, my voice trembling slightly. "When you asked me if I truly know what Paige is capable of, I wasn't entirely honest."

Zayn's eyes widen in surprise, but he remains silent, giving me the space to continue.

I sigh and continue, "My real name is Jada, and I... my life hasn't always been easy. I've been lost for a very long time. I guess you can say that I felt that I had to do things to survive, some things I'm not very proud of."

Tears well up in my eyes as I bare my truth. "Before I met you, Quinn approached me with an offer I felt I couldn't refuse. She offered to pay me one hundred thousand dollars to set up her husband and sleep with him. A few days after it was all said and done, Clay suddenly died."

His eyes widen with shock. "I can promise you that I had nothing to do with his death. But part of me deep down believes that Quinn tried to set me up."

As the weight of my confession settles between us, I shudder at the thought of what lies ahead. "Zayn, there's more," I say, my voice barely above a whisper. "Quinn, she's... she's dead too."

Zayn's eyes widen in shock once more, his grip tightening around me. "Dead? Stormy, what happened?" he asks, his voice laced with concern.

I swallow hard, the fear clawing at my throat. "It's Paige," I reply, the bitterness seeping into my words. "She's the one who's got me tied up in this mess."

Tears well up in my eyes as I bare my truth. "I'm scared, Zayn," I admit, my vulnerability unfiltered.

Zayn's expression darkens with anger, his jaw clenched tight. "You don't have to face this alone," he says firmly, his voice a steady anchor in the storm of my emotions. "We'll figure this out together, I promise."

Tears well up in my eyes as I bury my face in his chest, finding solace in his embrace. At that moment, with Zayn by my side, I feel a glimmer of hope.

ABOUT AN HOUR LATER, AS ZAYN'S MOTORCYCLE PULLS INTO THE garage, my heart races with anticipation and nerves. I take in the sight of his luxury sports car and another motorcycle, a silent testament to his adventurous spirit. His townhouse is sleek and modern, a reflection of his minimalist taste and wealth.

Entering his home, I'm struck by its simplicity yet undeniable elegance. It's a bachelor pad, but not in the stereotypical sense. Everything has its place, carefully curated without unnecessary excess. As I glance around, my eyes catch glimpses of Zayn's past captured in photographs displayed on the walls—him with his mom, in school, and during his time in the military.

As we settle into his living room, the tension crackles with an unspoken desire. Our lovemaking is wild and intense, leaving us both breathless and completely satisfied. Afterward, we drift into a peaceful slumber, cocooned in each other's arms. But as the night wears on, I'm jolted awake by a pressing urge to pee. Untangling myself from Zayn's hold, I slip out of bed, careful not to disturb his sleep, and grab one of his t-shirts before tiptoeing silently to the bathroom.

After using the toilet, I wander into the kitchen in need of water. My hands tremble slightly as I pour a glass, betraying the turmoil still swirling inside me. The cool liquid offers momentary relief, but my mind remains restless, haunted by the events of the last few weeks. I thought coming clean to Zayn would bring me some peace, but a part of me still feels unsettled, like something worse is lurking just around the corner.

Suddenly, the quiet of the night is broken by the sharp sound of glass shattering. My heart jumps in my chest as I look down to see the remnants of broken glass scattered across the floor. Cursing softly under my breath, I search for something to clean up the mess, my mind racing with a thousand thoughts. Following the trail of my clumsiness, I stumble upon a discreet door tucked away in a corner of the house. Intrigued yet hesitant, I push it open, my breath catching in my throat as I step into the room beyond.

What I find there leaves me frozen in shock, my mind racing to make sense of the disturbing scene. Before me is a large desk lined with monitors displaying live feeds from various locations, each one a window into a world of secrets and deception. The walls are covered with printed photos, each one carefully hung up, showing Paige, Gabrielle, and other faces I recognize from the party. My heart skips a beat when my eyes land on a picture of myself, hanging there unsuspecting, taken without my knowledge. A wave of violation washes over me, leaving me feeling exposed.

Confusion swirls within me, my head spinning from this unexpected revelation. As I turn to leave, my eyes fall upon a porcelain white mask reminiscent of the enigmatic figure from that party Halloween night. The memory of that chilling encounter floods back with startling clarity, sending a shiver down my spine.

My heart pounds, dread closing in like a tight grip, and fear washing over me. The safety I felt in Zayn's arms now seems far away, replaced by the looming threat that hides behind the walls of his once peaceful home.

Before I can fully process the implications of what I've discovered, Zayn walks in, his presence startling me. "I can explain," he begins.

I turn to him in shock, my eyes wide with disbelief. "What is this?" I whisper, my voice trembling with emotion.

"I was only trying to gather evidence to bring Paige down for killing my brother," he explains, his voice tinged with urgency.

His attempt to reassure me falls flat as anger and betrayal course through me. "And that included spying on me? Why?" I demand, my voice now trembling with anger and hurt.

"I needed to know who you were, and if you knew anything, that's it," he says, his tone guarded.

I am shocked by his confession.

Zayn's explanation only adds to my confusion, his words leaving me reeling with disbelief. "Then I saw you at the party that night, and I couldn't stay away from you. I never planned for things to go this far," he pleads, his voice filled with remorse.

"So this entire thing was a lie?" The words and realization form a knot in my throat.

"Stormy, I promise you everything I told you and shared with you was real. My feelings for you are real." He sighs, conflicted by his exposure. "But yes, at first, I didn't know if I could trust you until I did. We all have secrets, and these are mine," he explains, extending his arms in a gesture of openness.

But I refuse his embrace, pushing past him as I rush to gather my belongings. "Stay the fuck away from me," I hiss, my voice choked with emotion, consumed by a single thought—escape.

I dress in a hurry and rush out of his house and into the night; the world around me seems to blur into a haze of confusion and fear. Each step is a battle against the darkness closing in around me, the echoes of my own footsteps a haunting reminder of the danger lurking just beyond the shadows.

Betrayal floods my mind—Tempest, my mother, and now Zayn. Everyone I trusted has let me down. But before I can reach the safety of home, a new wave of fear grips me, sharp and sudden. I realize with a sinking feeling that I'm not alone. As I quicken my pace, I notice a dark car creeping along the curb, matching my every step. My heart races and panic sets in. They're following me. The realization sends a chill down my spine, amplifying the fear already gnawing at me. Suddenly, a dark figure emerges from the shadows, their intentions clear and menacing as they close in with eerie precision. In an instant, I break into a run, desperate to escape their pursuit.

Panic surges through me, adrenaline racing as I feel my stalker closing in. A hand suddenly grabs me, yanking me back. I struggle desperately, trying to break free, but it's too late—the world spins and blurs. Darkness swallows me whole as I fall into unconsciousness, my screams echoing into the silence until everything fades away.

CHAPTER

Twenty

GREAT REVELATIONS

Tempest

As the morning light filters through the curtains, I lie in bed, staring blankly at the chipped yellow paint on the wall. The peeling spots have always bothered me, but today, they seem to mock me, a constant reminder of everything falling apart in my life.

Jada's face flashes before me, her absence a dull ache that never seems to go away. Lance's words still echo in my mind, a painful reminder of all the broken relationships I've left behind. Work feels like a never-ending cycle of stress that I can't escape. But it's the memory of my miscarriage that hurts the most. The loss of a child, of a future that will never be, leaves me hollow and broken.

I rise out of my bed and start picking at the chipping paint, tears welling up as the memories flood in. Each piece of paint that falls to the floor is like a piece of my heart breaking off. I let the tears come, sobbing quietly as I scrape away at the wall, trying to find some release from the overwhelming sadness and despair.

But as I cry, another fear takes hold. I've spent so much of this year trying to heal, trying to piece myself back together. Now, it feels like all that hard work has been undone. I'm terrified that I'm back at square one, that all the progress I've made has been wiped away in a single, heartbreaking moment.

I reach for my phone, hands trembling, and quickly dial a number. As the phone rings, my heart races. When the voice on the other end picks up, I barely manage to get the words out.

"Hey, can you come over?" I whisper, my voice cracking. "I can't be alone right now."

After what feels like hours, the doorbell rings, pulling me out of my spiral. I drag myself to the door, opening it to find Fatima standing there. Her eyes widen as she takes in the state of me.

"Hey," she says softly, pulling me into a hug. "I'm so glad you called me, Temp. You don't have to go through this alone."

We sit on the couch with a box of pizza, and I finally let everything out. I tell her about my night with Lance, the drinking, the encounter with Jada, the stress from work, and the loneliness that's been crushing me. Fatima listens quietly, her concern growing with every word.

"I'm so sorry," she murmurs. "You've been carrying all this by yourself?"

"Yeah," I say, my voice shaky. "It's been a lot."

She squeezes my hand. "Well, I'm here, whatever you need."

As we talk, I start to feel a little lighter. Just having someone to share this with makes the burden a bit easier to bear. But then the conversation turns to Quinn's death, and the unease comes rushing back. Fatima shares my doubts about the supposed suicide, and we both know something doesn't add up.

Sitting across from her, my mind races as we go over the latest developments in the case. The article in front of us lays out a tangled web of connections between the city's elite and a much darker underworld.

"It just doesn't make sense. If Quinn killed Clay for a payout, why would she then turn around and kill herself?" I ask, frustration creeping into my voice.

Fatima shrugs. "Guilt, maybe?"

"Or someone's trying to clean up a mess they think she made," I say, my voice dropping to a whisper.

I hesitate, then finally reveal what's been weighing on me the most. "Jada is involved in this, Fatima. I'm sure of it. I need to get to the bottom of everything before she gets hurt. If these women are as dangerous as you say they are, I can't just sit back and do nothing."

Fatima's eyes widen in alarm. "Tempest, this is serious. You need to be careful."

"I know," I reply, feeling the weight of the situation pressing down on me. "But I have to help Jada. I can't just stand by and lose her."

"These women are dangerous and powerful," she warns, her concern evident.

I nod, appreciating her support. But there's no time to hesitate. Leaning forward, I lock eyes with Fatima, my voice firm. "Fatima, I need to know who your source is for this article. It could be the key to everything."

She hesitates, her brow furrowing. "Tempest, you know I promised them complete anonymity. I can't just break that trust."

"I get that," I say, my voice softening but still urgent. "But if I'm going to protect Jada, I need to know who we're up against."

Fatima's expression softens, conflicted but understanding. "This stays between us, Tempest. You have to promise me."

"I promise," I say without hesitation. "You have my word."

Fatima takes a deep breath, leaning in closer. "My source... it's Cherelle from the old neighborhood. She goes by Paige now," she confesses, the name hanging in the air like a ticking time bomb.

The moment the name leaves her lips, I feel like the ground beneath me just gave way. My mind reels, struggling to process what she's just said. Cherelle? Paige?

Fatima continues, her voice filled with concern and urgency. "Paige reached out to me a few months ago with a groundbreaking story that seemed almost too wild to be true. I didn't believe it at first, but she insisted it was real. She said she was scared for her life, Temp."

I draw in a sharp breath, the revelation hitting me hard. "Paige," I repeat, my mind racing.

I GRIP THE STEERING WHEEL, MY MIND RACING JUST AS FAST AS the car. Today feels different—like I'm finally going to break through the wall that's been keeping this case locked up tight. I can practically see the pieces falling into place, and I'm eager to get to the precinct, to dive in and figure it all out.

But as I drive, something tugs at me, pulling me off course. Before I know it, I'm turning down a street I haven't been on in a long time, a street I shouldn't be on. My heart starts to pound, and I tell myself I'm just checking in like I've done a few times before. But it's more than that. It's the guilt, the guilt that never really goes away, that's been eating away at me for so long now.

I slow down, scanning the familiar stretch of sidewalk until I see her—Mabel. She's sitting on a worn-out bench near the corner store, looking as tired as the day I first met her. I've driven by here before just to see if she was still hanging on, but today, for some reason, I can't just drive by. I can't just look and then turn away.

Today, I need to stop.

I pull over and park the car, my hands shaking a little as I step out. My feet feel heavy as I walk toward her, each step reminding me of the weight I've been carrying around for so long. When I'm close enough, Mabel looks up, and I can see the flicker of recognition in her eyes. There's surprise there, too, maybe even some resentment.

"Mabel," I say, my voice softer than I intended.

She looks me up and down, her expression guarded. "Tempest," she says, her voice rough, worn down by life.

The silence between us feels heavy, almost suffocating. I swallow hard, trying to find the right words, but they seem to elude me, like they always do.

"I know we haven't talked in a long time," I finally manage, my voice shaky. "But I wanted to see how you're doing."

Her eyes soften slightly, but the wariness remains. "Why now?" she asks, not accusing, just curious.

"I'm sorry for everything," I begin, my voice trembling with sincerity. "I know how much Jada loves you, how she's always loved you, and I just wanted to protect her. But I also understand the demons you face. I know how hard battling addiction can be. I'm so sorry that I judged you so harshly for it."

Mabel looks away, her gaze distant, lost in thought. The silence stretches out, and I start to worry she'll turn me away. But then she nods, slowly, deliberately. "Thank you," she says quietly.

"Let me help you, Mabel. Jada needs you," I say, holding my breath, hoping this is the start of making things right.

After what feels like an eternity, she finally says, "All right."

CHAPTER
Twenty-One

DIRTY AMBITIONS

Paige

Two years earlier…

I t wasn't supposed to be like this. When I married Dominic, I thought I knew exactly what I was getting into. Power, money, security—those were the things I craved, the things I needed to escape the life I had before. But somewhere along the way, I realized I wanted more. I wanted respect. I wanted love, or at least something resembling it. But Dom had other ideas.

He sits across from me at the dinner table, eyes glued to his phone, barely acknowledging my presence. I could be a piece of furniture for all he cares. The silence between us is suffocating, and I can't take it anymore.

"Dom," I say, trying to keep my voice steady. "We need to talk."

He doesn't even look up. "What now, Paige?"

The way he says my name, like it's an inconvenience, makes my blood boil. "I'm tired of being treated like this," I say, pushing the words out before I lose my nerve. "I'm not just some pretty thing you can parade around and ignore. I deserve respect. I deserve—"

His hand slams down on the table, finally pulling his eyes from his screen to glare at me. "Respect?" he spits out as he rises up from his chair, venom in his voice as he approaches me. "You think you deserve respect? You're nothing but a whore who uses her body to get ahead. Do you really think that I'm that naïve? That I didn't sniff out your true intentions? You used me, like I used you. You should be grateful I even looked your way."

The words hit me like a punch to the gut, but it's the actual slap that follows that sends me reeling. My cheek burns from the impact.

"Stay in your place," he sneers, his face twisted in contempt. "You're here to make me look good and keep your mouth shut. Don't forget that."

Tears well up in my eyes, but I refuse to let them fall. I won't give him the satisfaction, I've been humiliated enough.

The next morning, I end up at the spa, my sanctuary. The calming scent of eucalyptus and lavender greets me as I walk in, but today, it doesn't bring the usual comfort. I feel like a shell of myself, the weight of my marriage, of Dom's words, crushing me.

As I sink into the hot tub, letting the warmth envelop me, I feel the tears start to fall. I'm alone in every sense of the word. I've traded my soul for security, and now I have nothing to show for it but a life I hate and a husband who despises me.

After dressing, I find myself in the lounge, nestled in the spa, contemplating my next move. That's when I notice her. She's seated across the room, radiating confidence, her eyes sharp and her posture regal. She embodies everything I'm not—self-assured, powerful, in control. And she's looking right at me.

Our eyes meet, and it feels as though she's peering right into the depths of my soul. I can't look away. Compelled by her presence, I rise from my seat and approach her, desperate to get closer to the allure she exudes, hoping that whatever she possesses might rub off on me.

"Bad day?" she asks, her voice smooth and comforting, like silk against my skin.

I nod, my voice caught in my throat.

"I'm Gabrielle. Come," she says, beckoning me to sit and join her.

Without hesitation, I do just that, drawn to her like a moth to a flame. From that moment on, everything changes. With her help, I get rid of Dom. It's easier than I thought it would be. A little poison, a little manipulation, and soon, I'm free of him. But it's not enough. It's never enough.

Present Day

STANDING BEFORE THE MIRROR, I SCRUTINIZE EVERY ANGLE OF MY reflection, adjusting the sleek lines of my cocktail dress with a meticulous hand. I delicately apply my favorite blush, masking the deep-rooted insecurities that have clawed at my being for most of my life.

As I gaze at my reflection, memories flood my mind, transporting me back to my childhood, a time before the weight of expectations bore down upon me. Stormy and I fought bitterly as young girls, and I disappeared from that life, determined to transform myself completely. Now, I barely recognize the girl staring back at me in the mirror.

Plastic surgery became my salvation, a means to sculpt myself into the flawless image I had always longed to be. A new nose, enhanced breasts, a tummy tuck, and a new complexion—each procedure a step further from my old identity until Paige was born. My new look has helped me create a life I once only dreamed of—one filled with luxury, wealth, and privilege. I've worked relentlessly to break into this world, enduring men who repulsed me and marrying a man I couldn't stand. For so long, I thought that was the only way. Until I met Gabrielle Dubois.

Gabrielle showed me just how women could use their assets to secure their futures and get what they want at the demise of men, not merely with their dependence on them. I was ecstatic when she took me under her wing and introduced me to her social club. The Ebon Élite, a secret society of powerful widows who have turned their horrible marriages into a means to assume power and incredible wealth. Their influence extends far beyond their public personas, and their gatherings are the epitome of sophistication and secrecy. Full acceptance into this group would open doors and opportunities I never would've imagined, especially for a woman like me.

I've spent the first year of my affiliation going to extremes to prove my commitment and loyalty. In my personal quest for power, I've done everything I can to get closer to Gabrielle, doing her dirty deeds, even hosting that ridiculous charity gala. Yet, it still hasn't been enough to garner the respect and rank I know that I deserve. Instead, I am still disregarded and looked down upon as if I'm a nobody. I've played the game, and now I'm ready for more.

Unfortunately for Gabrielle and her followers, they've underestimated me. I've long despised people who think they are better than me. Gabrielle and her crew, with their smug attitudes and fake smiles, have gotten on my last nerve.

So, I fed Fatima the information for the exposé, hoping it would bring the heat onto the group and cause them to crumble from within. I wanted to see Gabrielle and the rest of those uppity bitches squirm, to watch their carefully constructed lives implode once the story caught the attention of the police. Fortunately, I was never fully accepted into their circle, so being a "nobody" would work in my favor.

Gabrielle's reign over this city has lasted far too long. It's time for a new queen bee. I am ready to challenge her, to take her throne, and take my rightful place as the ruler of this city's elite. For too long, I have lingered in the shadows, biding my time and waiting for the perfect moment to strike. But now, the waiting is over. The stage is set, and I am ready to take the crown.

Yes, Stormy's presence may complicate matters, but I refuse to let her stand in my way. She is nothing more than a pawn in my game, a means to an end. Although I hadn't anticipated Gabrielle taking such a liking to her so quickly. It makes me wonder what Stormy has that I don't. The thought is infuriating, as there would be no Stormy if it weren't for me. I practically made her in my image.

When I ran into her on that fateful day at the mall, she was just Jada, a true nobody. I sensed I'd finally gotten the upper hand. She was lost and curious about my lifestyle and the seeming Cinderella story. I used this to my advantage, knowing her exotic looks would capture the attention of powerful men. So, I took her under my wing, and Stormy was born. But over time, I have grown to once again loathe her distorted sense of superiority that has annoyed me since we were young girls.

I've come too far to allow Stormy, or anything else for that matter, to come in and derail my plan now, even though there have been some slight hiccups. I hadn't expected Quinn to turn around and get herself killed, just for following my advice on taking matters into her own hands. Or for my annoying brother-in-law to start snooping around, a problem that will need immediate attention.

I smile to myself, knowing that I will stop at nothing to claim my rightful place at the top, even if it means sacrificing everything I hold dear, including old acquaintances. As I don my armor and prepare for battle, a sense of determination washes over me. The time has come to seize control, rewrite the narrative of my life, and claim my destiny.

But first, there's tonight's dinner party—a gathering of the circle and my chance to secure my place at the top. As I fasten my heels, a surge of anticipation builds within me. Once dressed, I carefully slip the midnight-blue vial into my purse, a smile tugging at my lips. Tonight marks the beginning of my ascent to the throne.

CHAPTER
Twenty-Two

BLOOD AND LIBERATION

Stormy

A faint melody fills the air, instantly recognizable as my mother's favorite song, "The Sweetest Taboo," by the beautiful Sade. It's amazing how a simple tune can transport you back to forgotten days, flooding your mind with memories of warmth and simplicity.

In the mirror of my mind, I see my mother swaying to the rhythm of the music as she tended to our humble apartment. Though modest, it was our sanctuary, infused with the scent of Fabuloso that once permeated every nook and cranny. The smell, once overpowering, now brings a bittersweet sense of comfort and longing for my mother's embrace.

She was the embodiment of beauty in those moments, lost in her domestic rituals. My heart would swell with joy as she held me in her arms, and together, we'd dance and sing. Even now, the thought brings a warm, nostalgic sensation, though my attempts to join the song are thwarted by a gag, a cruel reminder of my current predicament.

Panic sets in as I struggle against my restraints, only to find a throbbing ache at the crown of my head. Uncertainty grips me as I attempt to make sense of my surroundings.

Suddenly, the door swings open, and a figure wearing a black mask and tailored suit stands before me. Wordlessly, he frees me from my restraints and points to a vintage dressing screen where a sleek black cocktail dress is hanging.

"Get dressed," his command is chillingly simple, accompanied by a stark warning against escape.

With trembling hands, I comply, shedding my clothes and slipping into the dress, feeling its smooth fabric against my skin. As I prepare myself at the vanity, my mind races with fear and determination, a silent vow to survive whatever awaits.

Once ready, my escort places my restraints back around my wrists, then leads me through the opulent mansion, the sounds of chatter growing louder with each step. I'm stunned when it hits me—I know this place. As I descend the grand staircase, the lavish surroundings bring back sharp memories of that Halloween night, when the women in golden masks moved through the shadows. Everything suddenly falls into place.

As we near a large set of double doors, my heartbeat quickens, bracing for what's to come. I hold my breath as my silent escort opens the doors. The grand dining room is bathed in the soft glow of candlelight, casting flickering shadows on the ornate walls. A long table is set with fine china and gleaming silverware, showcasing a feast of exotic dishes before the twelve women seated around it. At the head of the table, a woman in an intricate black gown and a gold-plated mask commands attention with her regal presence.

I'm led inside, my wrists bound, my skin hot with dread. The women's eyes follow me as I'm brought to the foot of the table and forced to sit down against my will, their expressions hidden behind their gilded masks.

"Ah, Stormy, dear. Welcome to my humble abode. I trust you're feeling... comfortable?" The voice, unmistakably Gabrielle Dubois, sends a chill down my spine.

"Gabrielle? Where am I? What do you want?" I manage, my voice trembling with fear.

With a chuckle, Gabrielle removes her mask, her expression both disarming and menacing. "Oh, my darling, it's not about what I want from you. It's about what we can offer you, should you choose to join us."

Realization dawns as I grasp the gravity of my situation. "The article, it's true."

"Yes," Gabrielle confirms, her smile betraying a sinister agenda. "We are The Ebon Élite—a powerful circle built on sisterhood and power. We have liberated ourselves from the constraints of marriage to seize control of our destinies."

I'm stunned, struggling to comprehend the magnitude of her revelation.

Gabrielle claps her hands, and the room falls silent. "Sisters," she begins, her voice carrying the weight of authority. "Tonight, we honor those before us and the sacrifices they made to ensure our freedom and power. We continue their legacy with a ritual that binds us and strengthens our cause."

A woman dressed in a deep crimson gown stands and approaches me, holding a silver chalice. She looks down at me with a mixture of pity and disdain before pouring a dark, viscous liquid into the cup. The metallic scent of blood fills the air, and I realize with horror what the chalice contains.

Gabrielle raises her arms, and the women around the table join hands, chanting in a language I don't understand. The haunting melody vibrates through the room, sending shivers down my spine. The crimson-clad woman offers the chalice to Gabrielle, who takes it with indifference.

She continues, her words dripping with both admiration and manipulation, "I've been watching you, Stormy. Your ambition and cunning are qualities I not only respect but admire. Join me, and together we can achieve greatness."

I'm left speechless, torn between fear and intrigue, as the truth of my situation sinks in.

CHAPTER
Twenty—Three

WHERE DANGER LURKS

Tempest

By nightfall, I arrive at Cherelle's building, my mind racing with questions about Quinn Winthrop's death and its ties to this secret widowed society. As I step into the luxury apartment building, it hits me—this was the setting of the gala I had scouted before. Flashing my badge to the receptionist, I head straight for the elevator, pressing the button for the top floor.

Riding up, my hands become clammy with anticipation. I'm shocked by Cherelle's—Paige's—involvement in all of this. Truth be told, I'd long since forgotten about her since our days as school-aged girls. Although I intentionally kept my distance from her, I remember Jada mentioning seeing her years ago. At the time, I thought it was just a chance encounter, but now I suspect it was much more.

As the elevator ascends, an uneasy realization begins to settle in—Jada may have kept more secrets from me than I'd like to admit. When the elevator bell rings, I step off and make my way toward her penthouse. But as I approach, I notice a commotion—a man frantically kicking and banging on Cherelle's door.

Concerned, I reach for my gun and proceed with caution. "Sir?"

The man turns to look at me, his eyes erratic. "Who are you?"

I open my coat, flashing my badge. "Philadelphia Police."

Suddenly, he looks relieved. "Oh, thank God." He turns to me, his expression wild with panic. "I believe my girlfriend is in danger."

I lower my gun. "Okay, slow down. Who is your girlfriend? Is she in the apartment?"

He places his hands on his hips and paces frantically. "No, no, this isn't her place. I don't even know how to explain this shit."

"Listen," I put my hand on his shoulder and encourage him to take a few deep, calming breaths. "I want to help you, but I can't if you don't tell me what's going on."

He lets out a heavy sigh, calming a bit and digging his hands into the pockets of his sweatpants. "Okay, did you read that article about the women who supposedly killed their wealthy husbands?" I nod, eager for him to continue. "I have reason to believe the article is true."

"Continue," I order.

"The women that she, my girlfriend, has been involved with—specifically, my sister-in-law. I believe they murdered my brother, and I think they have her."

"What is your girlfriend's name?" I ask.

"Stormy—wait, no, Jada," he explains.

My eyes grow big. "Jada?"

His eyebrow arches. "Yeah, you know her?"

My stomach drops, but I do my best to keep my composure. "Who is your sister-in-law?"

He digs his hands into his pockets. "Paige Hansen. She was married to my brother, Dominic Hansen."

I nod. "Okay, and you are?"

"Zayn. Zayn Ellis," he says.

"Listen to me, Zayn. Do you have any idea where Jada might be?" I ask.

He shakes his head. "No. We had a disagreement before she left my place. I saw her walking off last night."

"How? Did you chase after her? Or is there security surveillance?"

He nods quickly. "Yes, I have surveillance footage."

He pulls out his phone, and I watch with bated breath. A few moments pass before I see Jada walking out of his place; she appears to be irate. Then, a few seconds later, a car creeps up behind her, appearing to tread on her heels.

I quickly turn my attention back to Zayn. "You said you two had a fight. What was it about?" I inquire.

Frustration fills his eyes, "I don't see what that has to do with it. Look, something is wrong! I've been calling and texting her all day, even went by her place, but she's not there. She could be kidnapped or dead, for goodness' sake!"

"Zayn, listen. Calm down. I am here to help you," I say, assuring him while trying to keep a professional demeanor.

He rubs his temples. "I'd been running some secret surveillance on Paige, you know, for evidence, and Jada found some pictures. A couple of them she was in."

"So, she got upset and stormed out?" I ask.

He nods. Yes, that sounded like my sister.

"Were you able to get a license plate or anything?"

Zayn shakes his head, disappointed. "No, it was too dark to see."

My mind races as I process the information and the chilling realization that my sister is now seemingly a stranger. My biggest fear is coming to fruition before my eyes. If Jada is indeed in danger, there's no time to waste.

"Step aside, please," I instruct. "Go downstairs and get the receptionist up here immediately. I'll handle this," I say firmly.

I watch as he walks toward the elevator and disappears to get help. Turning back toward the door, I knock on it sharply, my senses on high alert as I wait for a response. But I am only met with silence. Distressed, I pull out my phone and promptly call Fatima.

"Hello?" she answers on the third ring, her voice groggy with sleep.

"Fatima, it's me. I need you to give me another name. I believe they have Jada," I say in rushed words, trying my best to remain practical.

"Temp, what do you mean?"

"Jada! I think they took her," I yell. "Cherelle is more involved in this than you think. Please, give me something. She could be in real danger."

My voice trembles as reality begins to settle in. I can't bear the thought of losing another person that I love.

"Okay, I'll call you right back," she says, her voice more alert now.

We hang up, and as I wait and pace, moments later, Zayn returns with a building attendant. They use a spare key to unlock the door.

"Mrs. Hansen, Philadelphia Police," I announce with my gun drawn as we make our way through the apartment. But it's eerily empty.

Suddenly, my phone rings, and I pick up. "Hey."

"Gabrielle Dubois. Paige said she set this whole thing in motion and created the society."

"Gabrielle Dubois. Got it. Thank you," I hang up.

Zayn speaks up. "What is it?"

"We have to go," I say and promptly put in a call with dispatch, requesting the last known address of Gabrielle Dubois.

At my car, I pull on the latch to open my door, and as I do, dispatch provides the details. "823 Moonlight Road."

I hop into the car and turn to Zayn. "Get in."

He does as he's told, and I turn on my police siren, speeding to the Dubois residence and hoping that I'm not too late.

CHAPTER
Twenty-Four

TRUTHS & LIES

Stormy

My heart and mind race as I search for a way out of this predicament. The group of women rise from their seats, and I twist in my seat under the pressure of my captor's grip. "Let me go, you're all crazy!" I shout, but my pleas fall on deaf ears.

Gabrielle raises her arms, and the women around the table join hands, chanting in a language I don't understand.

"Blood of the innocent, blood of the betrayed," Gabrielle announces, lifting the chalice high. "With this sacrifice, we renew our pact and pledge our loyalty to the sisterhood."

The women around the table echo her words, their voices rising in unison. I watch, horrified, as they all drink the blood. Gabrielle uses her pinky to gently wipe the corner of her mouth.

She approaches me, holding the chalice out. "Join us, Stormy. Drink," she commands, her eyes locking onto mine. "Embrace your fate and join us in our quest for power."

Horrified, I look around the room at the women who have shaped the shadows of this city. My life has been a series of struggles and betrayals, and here is an opportunity to turn the tables. Despite the betrayal and the dangers, a spark of determination ignites within me.

Before I can respond, a familiar voice cuts through the tension. "You've got to be fucking kidding me," a voice hisses. The woman in the crimson-colored dress steps forward. I watch, stunned, as she rips the golden mask from her face—it's Paige. She stares at me with fury in her eyes. "What has she done to earn her place? She doesn't belong here!"

Gabrielle's gaze shifts to Paige, a hint of annoyance flickering in her eyes. "Paige, your jealousy is unbecoming."

My heart pounds as the pieces fall into place. "You... you are involved in this?" The realization settles that she did, in fact, kill her husband. "Paige, oh my God, what have you done?" I say, my voice trembling with a mix of rage and realization.

Paige sneers. "What do you think, Stormy? Of course I did, and I'd do it again! And what about you? A pathetic thieving whore that still has the nerve to think you're better than me? Look at what I've done! Look at how far I've come! You'd be nothing if it weren't for me."

I stare at her in pure disgust, dumbfounded by her cold-bloodedness.

Gabrielle raises her hand, silencing Paige. "Enough. This is not about your past grievances."

Paige cuts her eyes at Gabrielle, the wrath of her fury far from exhausted, "Don't tell me what to do, bitch. Your time is through," she says. She slams her hand onto the table. "After everything that I've done to prove myself to you, doing your bidding, ensuring all the loose ends are tied up—you're just going to let her in? You're a tired old bitch that's a fraud. I know your story, Gabrielle. A model from Paris, huh? You're nothing but trash from South Philly." Her voice rises, echoing through the grand ballroom.

Gabrielle's eyes strain, a clear indication of her intolerance for being challenged. She fixes her gaze on Paige, her demeanor apathetic. As she approaches her challenger, she crosses her arms in front of her chest, meeting her toe to toe, "Don't get cute. I let you into our world, and I can most certainly take you out. There's a reason I haven't fully let you join us, Paige. You're delusional, untrustworthy, and, most of all, desperate. You'll never be me. Not even on your best day."

Paige bristles at the thinly veiled criticism, her eyes flashing with defiance. "I've done what was necessary to secure my position," she retorts, her voice dripping with venom.

Gabrielle's smile turns wicked. "Ah, but at what cost, Paige? Loyalty is a rare commodity, and your actions have cast doubt upon your allegiance. We know that it was you who leaked the information to that article. And I know that you tried to poison us all tonight."

The group mutters, seemingly angry. Paige's eyes widen in fear as the gravity of her situation sinks in; her mask seemingly has been ripped off, and her true intentions revealed.

"You see, Paige, I've been on to you for quite some time. I knew one day you'd try to come in here and take my spot. I just wasn't sure just how far you'd be willing to go. I planned to make you answer for your crimes after dinner, of course, but now seems fitting," she explains.

Paige, once confident and unrelenting, now appears to be petrified. She knows that she's about to face a punishment that will be witnessed by all.

Gabrielle addresses the group, "Ladies, as you know, we hold ourselves to the highest standards of conduct. And when one of our own strays from the path, it is our duty to ensure that justice is served."

I sit there frozen, fearful of what's to come.

Gabrielle continues, "Paige, you have violated one of our most sacred rules. Your reckless behavior has put the sisterhood at risk, and for that, you must be held accountable. You must be eliminated, just as we eliminated Quinn."

Before Paige can respond or run, Gabrielle's associate frees my shoulders from his grip and steps forward, a silent figure in the dimly lit room. With a swift motion, he snaps Paige's neck, the sound echoing through the chamber.

Shock reverberates through my veins as Paige's lifeless body slumps to the ground. In the stunned silence that follows, Gabrielle's voice rings out, cold and unwavering. "Let this be a lesson to all who would betray The Ebon Élite. Loyalty above all else."

Gabrielle looks at me. "Now, my dear, it appears we've just gotten a new opening in our group. You have two options. You can either cooperate and join our ranks, or... well, let's just say the alternative isn't very appealing, as you can see."

As the women begin to chant again, my mind races, knowing that whatever choice I make will shape the course of my fate. My life flashes before my eyes. How I wish I could turn back and lead a different life. Visions of my mother flash before me, fearful that I'll never see her again. My sister Tempest's face fills my mind, and I instantly regret holding onto the weight of the grudge that I've carried with me all this time. I miss her. I think of Zayn and how I wish I could be back at his place with him, ready to work through our pasts and start fresh.

A tear streams down my face as I realize that day will likely never come. Gabrielle approaches me, untying one of my hands from the chair, then picks up my chalice, and hands it to me. My hands shake as I take it, the metallic tang of blood filling my nostrils. The room seems to close in around me, the chanting growing louder, more insistent. I can feel the weight of their expectations pressing down on me, the pressure to comply almost overwhelming.

But as I raise the chalice to my lips, something inside me rebels. I can't be a part of this. I can't give in to their twisted rituals. I glance around the room, searching for an ally, for any sign of help. My eyes meet Gabrielle's, and for a moment, I see a flicker of sadism in her gaze.

With a sudden surge of defiance, I throw the chalice to the ground, the blood splattering across the pristine tablecloth. The chanting stops abruptly, and a shocked silence fills the room. Gabrielle's expression hardens, her eyes narrowing with fury.

Gabrielle steps back, her face full of cold rage. "Very well," she says, her voice like ice. "If you won't join us willingly, then you will serve as an example to those who might deny us."

She nods to the associate to deliver the same punishment as he'd previously inflicted on Paige. I take a deep breath and calm myself, prepared to meet my fate. Then suddenly, to my surprise, the doors to the dining room burst open. "Freeze!"

I'm stunned to see my sister, flanked by the Philadelphia Police, descend into the room, guns drawn. Tempest keeps her eyes on me as she steps forward before shifting her gaze to Gabrielle and her followers.

"You're under arrest," she declares, her voice ringing with authority as she places handcuffs on Gabrielle's wrists.

CHAPTER
Twenty-Five

NEW DETERMINATION

Tempest

One year later…

I sit in the plush leather armchair of Dr. Nelson's office, the familiar scent of lavender and aged books surrounding me. The soft, ambient lighting creates a calming atmosphere, a stark contrast to the chaos I've faced recently. Dr. Nelson, with her kind eyes and patient demeanor, sits across from me, a notepad in hand.

"Tempest, it's good to see you again," Dr. Nelson begins, her voice soothing. "How have you been holding up since the last time we spoke?"

I glance over her shoulders into the eyes of the twisted woman that haunted me before. I take a deep breath, the weight of recent events heavy on my shoulders. "It's been... intense, to say the least. But I'm good, great, actually."

Dr. Nelson raises an eyebrow, intrigued. "That's the first time I've heard you talk like that. What changed?"

I nod. "Me, I guess. I decided to finally forgive myself, you know? And like you said, I'm just taking it one day at a time."

"Cracking a major case feels good, too, I'm sure." She winks.

A smile covers my face, "Yes, that too. We've officially brought charges against all the women in the group. It's still so unbelievable. They were made up of the widows of prominent judges, politicians, oil tycoons, and real estate developers. It's been a whirlwind, to say the least."

Dr. Nelson scribbles a few notes before looking up. "I can only imagine." She takes her glasses off, looking at me. "You said that you managed to forgive yourself after all this time. What brought that on?"

I sigh, a hint of a smile playing on my lips. "This case, surprisingly. It helped me to reunite with my sister and come to terms with some things in my past. We're not as close as we once were, but we're working on it. She's forgiven me, and that's all I ever wanted. This whole ordeal made us realize how much we need each other, oddly enough. She's been through so much, and I realize now how much I've missed having her in my life. We're just taking it one step at a time."

"That's good to hear," Dr. Nelson says, genuinely pleased. "And how are you coping with everything personally? The stress of the case, the danger, the emotional toll?"

I pause, considering my words carefully. "It's been tough. There were moments when I thought I wouldn't make it through. But having a sense of purpose, knowing that I'm making a difference, that helps. And... talking to you helps too."

Dr. Nelson smiles warmly. "I'm glad I can be of help. It's important to take care of yourself, especially when dealing with such high-stress situations. Have you been doing anything in particular to unwind or relax?"

"I just finished renovating my house. That kept me pretty busy," I admit. "And yoga on Sundays with Fatima and boxing classes during the week."

"That's excellent," Dr. Nelson encourages. "Routine can be very grounding."

We spend the next few minutes talking and discussing my future plans and what lies ahead. As we talk, I can't help but think about the changes in my life recently. After months of friendly banter and harmless flirting, I finally agreed to give love another try and started dating Andre, the owner of the boxing gym I go to. His easygoing nature and quiet confidence drew me in, and I realized I was completely over Lance, who's now married. It feels good to open up to someone new and give love a try.

At the end of my session, Dr. Nelson gives me some encouraging words, "Well, I haven't seen you this optimistic at the end of a session, Tempest. I love this for you."

I nod, feeling a sense of calm I haven't experienced in a long time. "Thank you, Dr. Nelson. For everything."

Dr. Nelson places her notepad on the table and leans forward slightly. "Remember, it's okay to lean on others. You're not alone. You've been through a lot, and it's perfectly normal to need support. You're doing an incredible job, both professionally and personally. Be proud of yourself, Tempest."

"I am," I say with a smile.

As I leave the therapy session, I feel a renewed sense of strength and clarity. The path ahead is still uncertain, but for the first time in a long while, I feel ready to face whatever comes next.

CHRISTMAS EVE, THE EVENING IS COLD AS WINTER FLURRIES begin to fall. I step into the cozy little restaurant. The soft hum of conversations and the clinking of cutlery create a comforting background noise. The smell of Italian cuisine fills the air, and for a moment, I'm transported back to simpler times. My eyes scan the room until they land on Jada, sitting at a corner table, nervously fidgeting with the napkin in her lap.

Taking a deep breath, I make my way over to her. As I approach, she looks up, her eyes meeting mine with a mixture of apprehension and hope. "Hey, Temp," she says softly, standing to give me a hug.

"Hey, Jada," I reply, returning the hug warmly. We both sit down, and a moment of awkward silence follows as we look over the menus.

After a few moments, I decide to break the ice. "How have you been holding up?"

Jada sighs, setting the menu aside. "It's been rough. Preparing to testify, dealing with everything that's happened... it's a lot to process."

"I can only imagine," I say, my voice gentle. "But you're incredibly brave for doing this. Your testimony is going to make a huge difference, if it comes to that."

"What do you mean?" she asks with her brow raised.

"I just got off the phone with Lance, who is leading the prosecution. He just told me that he struck a deal, and he was able to get a confession from Gabrielle's assistant, Silas Black-wood. We're hoping his cooperation will force the others to do the same," I say, my voice tinged with exhaustion.

She lets out a heavy breath, a sense of relief washing over her. "Thank goodness." Then her eyes grow big, and she leans forward. "Wait, Lance, as in, Lance, Lance?"

I nod. Upon our reconciliation, I've spent time catching her up on all that's happened over the last two years, the mis-carriage, the breakup, and my time in rehab, "Yeah, girl, that Lance."

"You're so strong to be able to even work with him after everything," she says with a hint of admiration.

"Tell me about it. It's weird, one day I decided I was done giving him power over me, and it was done like that," I say with a snap of my fingers to emphasize the swiftness of the switch.

"I'm sure it doesn't hurt having that fine ass man keeping you company, too," she teases, and we both laugh.

Just then, a waiter approaches, and we order our meals. She orders a glass of wine while I settle on a Diet Coke. As we wait, the conversation turns to lighter topics—memories from our childhood, funny stories, and dreams we once had. For the first time in a long while, it feels like we're reconnecting, finding the sisterly bond we once had.

"How are things with Zayn?" I ask as I take a sip of my soda.

"Really good, it's kind of scary. We're going away for New Years. Dubai, I think, he said it's a surprise," she reveals.

"Dubai? Wow, that's exciting!"

Her eyes light up. "I can't wait. He's really good to me, you know, besides the whole spying thing."

We giggle, and then I say, "Hey, in other circumstances, I'd tell you to run for the hills, but in this case, his commitment to bringing justice for his brother's death was pretty admirable."

As the waiter brings our food, I decide it's time to address the heavier matters. I reach into my bag and pull out a small envelope, sliding it across the table to Jada. "I have something for you."

Her brow furrows in curiosity as she takes the envelope and opens it. Inside is the thumb drive containing evidence Quinn had of Jada with Clay. Her eyes widen in shock and then fill with gratitude. "What's this?"

I nod. "I thought you should have them, I shredded the printouts. They're evidence, yeah, but they're also a piece of your life that you can keep private if you want. You have a chance to start fresh, and I don't want anything from the past weighing you down. Besides, we've got plenty more evidence tied to that crazy organization."

Tears glisten in her eyes as she looks up at me. "Thank you, Temp. This really means a lot."

"How's Mabel doing? She's been clean for, what, a year now?"

Jada nods with pride. "Yeah, she's really sticking with it this time. I'm so proud of her. I can't thank you enough for what you did for her, by the way. Taking her to rehab, paying for her recovery. For some reason, whenever I'd offer she'd reject it, so you have no idea how much this means to me."

I give a small smile, feeling the weight of our past slowly lifting. "I needed to make amends, Jada. I couldn't just stand by and do nothing."

We continue eating, the mood lighter now that some of the heaviness has lifted. Jada shares her plans for the future and how she wants to take acting classes and see the world.

"So, now what?"

I chew on my food for a moment and contemplate her question, "Karina Allegro."

Her brow arches, "What?"

"Karina Allegro, it's a cold case. I'm going to solve it. Unfortunately, there are more sickos out there that need to be stopped."

Jada nods, "And you're just the woman for the job."

As we finish our meal, I reach across the table and take her hand. "I'm really proud of you, Jada. We've both come such a long way."

She nods in agreement. "We sure have."

"I know we're still working on things, but I'm here for you, whatever you need," I add.

She squeezes my hand, a tear sliding down her cheek. "I'm proud of you too, Temp. I've missed you so much. Let's promise not to let anything come between us again."

"Promise," I say, my voice firm with determination.

The End!

ACKNOWLEDGMENTS

THIS BOOK WOULD NOT HAVE BEEN POSSIBLE WITHOUT THE SUPport, inspiration, and encouragement of so many wonderful people.

To those who brainstormed with me, allowed me to bounce countless ideas off them, and listened patiently as I explored plot twists and character arcs — thank you for being my sounding boards and creative partners. Your insights, feedback, and belief in my vision have been invaluable.

To everyone who generously gave their time for interviews, shared their knowledge, and offered their perspectives — I am deeply grateful. Your contributions have added depth and authenticity to this story.

And finally, to my family, friends, and loved ones who have been there through every draft, every rewrite, and every moment of doubt — thank you for your unwavering support, love, and encouragement. You've lifted me up when I needed it most and celebrated every victory, big or small.

This book is as much yours as it is mine.

ABOUT THE AUTHOR

Monique Elise is a Philadelphia-based, four-time self-published author and a proud graduate of Temple University. Known for her vibrant storytelling and empowering messages, Monique believes that women can have it all and be unapologetically fabulous while doing so.

Since making her debut in 2017 with the compelling 3-part series "Dilemmas of a Damsel," Monique has captivated readers with her tales of black love and resilience. Her latest novel, "Red Echo," soared to the top of the Amazon charts, becoming a #1 Bestseller in her genre during the summer of 2020. With four novels to her name and a fifth dropping this fall, Monique continues to push the boundaries of her creative talents and compelling tales.

Monique Elise is more than an author; she is a beacon of empowerment for women everywhere. Her commitment to inspiring others through storytelling encourages her readers and followers to embrace their dreams with confidence and style.

Discover more about Monique and her journey at www. moniqueelise.com.

Explore My Other Novels!

Connect with Me!